~SWEPT FROM THE SHALLOWS~

Book One

Amanda Summers
Kay Summers

SON OF THUNDER PUBLICATIONS

Published by Son of Thunder Publications, Ltd., 2018
www.sonofthunderpublications.org

Cover art by David Munoz

Edited by Rachel L. Hall

Book Layout ©2017 BookDesignTemplates.com,
with additional elements by Rachel L. Hall.

Swept from the Shallows, Book One: Aven on Earth /
Amanda Summers and Kay Summers. —1st ed.

Published in the United Kingdom for world-wide distribution.

ISBN 978-1-731638-4-3 Paperback
ISBN 978-911251-26-2 Hardback
ISBN 978-1-911251-27-9 Kindle and eBook

We would like to dedicate this book first and foremost to Christos, The Anointed One, without whom we would have no access to the Father.

We honor Grandpa Bill and Joe who have greatly impacted our lives. We also honor those who have gone before us.

To Kirsten, Dan, Jocelyn and Eli who brought to our attention a need for children's books. Your encounters with Christos inspire us.

To Breeze who gave us a tweenager's perspective and feedback.

To Heather, MaryLynn, and everyone else at Son of Thunder Publications who encouraged us to write. This book would not have been written without you.

Last but not least, we would like to dedicate it to every reader who is brave enough to believe that through Christ all things are possible. It is our sincerest prayer for you that you would:

Walk away from the shallows
In which men wade—
Forsake them for the depths
Of the deep.

Embrace your chance to be
Swept away—
And thus from your fears
Find release.

Contents

Aven on Earth

CHAPTER 1

Heaven Sent

LAUGHTER FILLED THE ATMOSPHERE as children splashed about in the river. Dolphins leapt into the air and did aerial tricks as other children watched with glee. The water, not to be outdone, began splashing and dancing, throwing itself about and wetting the sand on the soft banks of the river. The waterfall sang as it poured over the cliffs, rejoicing on its journey. Parrotfish, angelfish, and butterfly fish—just to name a few of the bright, colorful creatures that graced this area—

played along the shoreline, teasingly nipping at the children's toes.

"Aven," Liam said, turning to the little girl sitting closest to him on the bank, "race you to the bottom!"

"You're on!" Aven jumped up, only too happy to dive into the crystal waters. She didn't know why they ever bothered to race. It didn't matter who won. It was always Liam—this was something he was better at. He was strong and almost never sat still. Aven, on the other hand, was much more of a gentle spirit. She could often be found lying on her back, staring at the sky through the leaves or talking to the lions and other creatures as they bathed in the light. She was always up for an adventure, too, but it was so peaceful here she found contentment in just being still.

"I won!" Liam shouted from a healthy distance. "Want to explore while we're down here?"

"Why do you think I came?" Aven teased. Something shiny caught her eye. "What's that?"

The children swam over to the shiny object Aven had seen out of the corner of her eye. It was a sapphire—a beautiful, deep blue, perfectly teardrop-shaped, massive sapphire!

"Aren't sapphires your favorite?" Liam asked Aven.

"Yes, they are! Blue is my favorite color." She picked up the gem that was about the size of a large acorn. "I know just what I'm going to do with it." She took off her red sash and made a little bag out of it. Placing the sapphire in the bag, she tied it around her waist and continued to swim.

The current the children made while swimming along the bottom stirred up the soft white sand of the river bed, revealing the vast treasures scattered along the reef. Gold and silver—along with far too many gems to count—lay uncovered. The uncovered treasure caught the light and began to shine.

"Lie on your back," Aven instructed Liam as she gracefully twisted about and settled herself to rest on the soft floor. Liam, not quite as gracefully, followed her lead and plopped himself next to her.

"Look up," Aven said.

"Wow!" was the only response Liam could muster.

As the treasure caught and then reflected the light from above, the water lit up with color. The creatures swimming cast ripples through the water causing the colors to dance about. They watched as purple, blue, green, red and every other color of the rainbow beamed and shot up like stage lights landing like spotlights on different creatures. Every now and then a silver dolphin or shark would swim over them, the light would reflect against their silver skin making them look like they were changing colors.

As Aven lay there watching the magnificent scene unfold, she shivered with delight wondering if her existence could possibly get any better.

Leaving the rest of the treasure behind, Aven surfaced with the sapphire that had caught her attention out of the corner of her eye. It was the only one that had called out to her.

Taking the sapphire with her, she waved to Liam as she skipped into the trees. Coming upon a clearing, she found what she'd been looking for—it was a beautiful herd of horses.

"Hello, Aven."

She turned to see one of her best friends coming towards her. "Flash, I was looking for you," she said to the dapple-gray colt who was now at her side. "Can you take me to the Sea of Glass?"

"Sounds fun," Flash said, turning so Aven could climb onto his back. "Hold on!"

When they arrived at the Sea of Glass, Flash leaned down to let Aven slip off. She walked a short distance away so she could be on her own for a moment. Kneeling down, she placed her hand on the Sea and said a quick prayer: "Papa, today I found this sapphire. It called out to me, asking me to pick it up. Sapphires are my favorite. You have given me everything I need. Thank

You for allowing me to find this sapphire. I give it back to You."

With that, she dropped the sapphire into the Sea.

Aven was resting behind the waterfall when she heard a voice excitedly announce, "Christos is headed to The Tree!"

Aven jumped out from behind the flowing water to get a better view. Christos was so awesome! She watched as He rode Lightning in perfect harmony. It was like they were one. The ground shook as Lightning's hooves hit the ground, causing a stir, waking everything up that may have been sleeping, and calling everyone who may have been wandering back.

Kids and creatures of all kinds appeared as if out of nowhere and suddenly The Tree found itself at the center of an excited gathering. Christos dismounted Lightning and walked to The Tree, sitting down where He always sat. As Christos leaned against the trunk, energy surged from Him into The Tree which then began to shimmer and come to life. Its leaves rustled and the branches seemed to reach towards Christos, as if to embrace Him. The Tree rejoiced as colors swept through it in a brilliant light display. No matter how many times Aven saw this spectacle, it sent shivers through her body as she felt drawn into the energy resonating from Christos, through The Tree, and touching her heart. This oneness was divine.

"Aven," she heard Christos say. "Aven!"

That was her. Christos was calling her! It was her turn. Finally, she was ready. Finally, she was off to a new adventure. But did she want to go? She loved this place and had always felt peace and joy here. She was safe, she was loved, she was a part of everyone and everything, and everyone and everything was a part of her. This was her home, it was where she belonged. But now it was time to decide her destiny. She had been chosen!

Aven ran to Christos Who pulled her onto His lap. For a moment she laid her head against His chest, allowing her being to come into agreement with His heart.

"Aven," Christos said again, pulling her back so He could look into her eyes. "Will you do something for Me?" He asked.

"Of course!" Aven replied without hesitation. She knew she could trust Christos with every fiber of her being. "What is it?"

"I have chosen you to journey to the Realm of Earth at this time. Earth itself is now groaning for the manifestation of My children. You have been saved for this time, you are called to be My child.

Will you go and manifest My Kingdom in that Realm?"

Aven knew she had a choice. Part of her wanted to stay, but she had seen people return after their journey in the Earth Realm, and they had been changed, transformed. They looked much more like Christos. They had matured and had a special place in the Kingdom. They had done Christos a great service, and she had heard Christos say, "Well done!" to them. Aven wanted to hear those words more than anything. She wanted to be a part of Him in ways she hadn't known and she knew that the only way to be closer to Him than she was, was to complete this journey.

"I will go," Aven said.

Christos smiled at her, then looked up into The Tree. As she followed His gaze she saw something she'd never noticed before. She'd seen Christos feed others fruit—fruit that looked delicious, sweet, and juicy—but until now she had never seen where this fruit came from. As she stared into The Tree, she realized that it was growing scrolls.

"Aven, look at Me," Christos commanded, gently turning her face to meet His gaze. "There is a family in the Earth Realm in need of the love and joy you carry. Will you choose a life with this family? Will you go and bring love and joy to them?"

As Aven looked into Christos' eyes she could see the family He was asking her to choose. It felt as though in one moment the entire family history flashed before her eyes and she knew them and she instantly loved them. "Christos," she began, longing to please Him, "you know what is best for me. I trust You and I will love this family. I will do my best to bring them joy."

"I love you," Christos replied, taking a moment to let Aven absorb the weight of His love.

Carefully, He picked a scroll from The Tree and began telling her what it truly means to be a Child of God, to rule and reign. He told her things she'd never heard before, things about who she really was. As He did, the scroll began to glow with a golden light.

When He was done speaking, He turned the scroll over in His hand. It became like the delightful fruit she had seen so many times before. He handed it to Aven to eat. As she took a bite, juice dripped down her chin. Aven tingled as she was overwhelmed with love, peace and joy.

As she ate, Christos told her that everything she needed for her journey in the Earth Realm was in this fruit and had now become a part of her. Everything she could ever need was growing inside of her. As she watered the seeds she had just consumed, they would grow. They would become whatever she needed. "Are you ready?" Christos asked, looking into the depths of Aven's being.

"I am," Aven replied, knowing she was, yet, somehow still longing to stay with Him. To be closer to Him.

Christos stood up and carried her to the side of The Tree. He knelt and placed His hand on the ground. As He did, a blue light began to pierce the earth and a portal opened before her eyes.

Christos took her hand. Looking her in the eye He said, "Remember what I told you. There are things in the Earth Realm that will try to make you forget who you are. Other things will even try to steal and change your identity. This is the only real threat you will face there. As long as you remember who you are, you will be safe. *I AM*, and you are a part of me, so *YOU ARE*."

With that, Aven stepped into the portal and everything changed.

CHAPTER 2

The Cave

"WHERE AM I?" Aven wondered as she tried to move to take in her surroundings. This wasn't home. This wasn't like anything she'd ever known and this certainly couldn't be where Christos had meant to send her. He would never put her in such a place. She was supposed to be with a family she loved. Not here. She didn't even know where "here" was.

As she began to realize the situation she was in, she looked frantically for a way out. The light from the portal was beginning to fade. Desperately, Aven reached towards the light as it disappeared. Everything in her longed to go back, but something she couldn't see was holding her. It was like she was being knit to something and was now tied to this place.

"How could this have happened?" Aven wondered as the full weight of the darkness settled around her. She was alone. She was cold. And for the first time in her existence she was afraid, she was very afraid.

As Aven began to settle into her new home, she started noticing things she hadn't before. While she couldn't see much here in this new place, she could still feel. She learned to pay attention to what she felt, and as she did, she could feel more and more.

She could feel people around her. She still missed Christos, but she was starting to love the people she felt. She only wished she could interact with them. Aven wasn't afraid anymore, but she was still lonely.

"Hello, sis!"

Startled, Aven turned to see who had spoken. To her dismay, she was still alone.

The voice came again. "Can you hear me, sis?"

Aven wasn't sure who was speaking to her, but she wasn't going to miss out on an opportunity to talk to someone. Anyone! "Yes, I can hear you," she replied excitedly.

"I knew you were in there. I told Mom, but she didn't believe me."

"I've been here for ages! Where am I? And who are you?"

"You're in Mom's tummy. I don't really understand it yet, but what I do know is that Christos sent you here from Heaven, and that's where we all begin our journey in the Earth Realm."

"Christos! You know Christos?" Aven couldn't believe her ears! Someone who knew her Best Friend, right here speaking into this dark abyss she was in.

"Of course I know Christos. I'm Joe, by the way. I'm your big brother. I came from Heaven just like you did. I've been here for three years, so I know what you're going through. I knew you were coming at some point. I've been waiting to show you around. I can't wait until you can come out and play."

"What is it like where you are?" Aven asked, excited to hear she wouldn't be stuck where she was forever.

"Oh, you'll love it. We live in Wassaic, New York. It's a lot like home. Christos comes to play every day. Plus, I'm here to look out for you. It's my nap time so I need to go, but I'll be back to talk soon," Joe assured Aven.

Hope filled Aven's little heart as Joe said goodbye. She couldn't wait to speak to him again. She had so many questions to ask. To think that all this time, she had a brother who loved her and wanted to spend time with her. She wasn't alone after all. To top it all off, Christos visited Joe every day! She longed to escape this limbo and see what came next.

True to his word, Joe wasn't gone long. It was wonderful having someone to talk to, someone to answer her questions. According to Joe, her Mom, Lily, and Dad, David—along with other people—tried talking to her, too. She guessed those were the random noises she heard. But she couldn't understand them like she understood Joe. Joe was usually around, though, and he'd translate for her. It was usually silly things like, "Hello, baby girl!" or "How's the baby girl?" How did they think she was? She could barely move, things were changing every day, and Joe was the only one who could understand her. She was so thankful for Joe.

"Aunt Celeste is coming home!" Joe practically bounced out of his skin as he told Aven this news.

Aven had learned how to read emotions over the last few months. Her relationship with Joe had helped her out a lot with that. She had always known what she had felt but she hadn't known what to call her feelings. She could also tell how the people around her were feeling and Joe had helped her learn to trust herself. She was almost always right. She still didn't understand everything she felt but knew a lot more than she had a few months ago. This emotion coming from Joe was a mixture of pure joy and excitement. Aven couldn't wait to learn more.

"Who's Aunt Celeste? Why are you so excited?" Aven asked Joe, not even trying to hide her confusion and delight.

"She's my favorite aunt!" Joe replied, hugging their mom's stomach so Aven could feel him even closer.

"What's an aunt?"

"Remember how I told you you're my sister and what that means?"

"Yes."

"Remember what I told you about moms and dads?"

"Yes." Aven was happy to realize just how much she already knew.

"Well, an aunt is a mom or dad's sister. Aunt Celeste is my favorite! She's so much fun and she has always understood me. I could talk to her way before I could talk to anyone else. She's been in Texas for a few months training a horse for show jumping. She wants to train horses for the Olympics, that's her dream. She's the best. I missed her so much. It feels like she's been gone forever. I can't wait to see her. Just wait—you'll love her, too."

Aven tried to listen to Joe as he continued to tell her about their Aunt Celeste and all the exciting things she did, but her mind was spinning. She'd just started to feel like she could really understand Joe, but this was gibberish. Where was Texas? What was a month? What was a horse? What were the Olympics? At least one thing was perfectly clear: Joe was excited.

All the excitement had tired Aven out and she decided to take a nap while waiting for the amazing Aunt Celeste.

"Ouch!" Aven said, awakening with a start. What was that? It felt like an electric shock had zapped her. It hadn't hurt exactly, but it was quite the surprise for Aven. As Aven looked, she could see white light approaching her.

"Hello, my love. It's so nice to finally meet you."

Aven didn't say a word. She was completely filled with love and joy. She felt warmth like she hadn't felt since leaving Heaven. She didn't want the moment to end.

"I'm your Aunt Celeste. I can't wait till you're born so I can hold you in my arms," Celeste told Aven, sensing her contentment as well as her confusion.

Aven pressed herself into the light, allowing the love to completely fill her. Aven was too filled with joy for words. She could hear voices in the distance and the peace she felt as she lay there carried her into a deep sleep filled with dreams of home.

"So, was I right? I was, huh? Aunt Celeste is the best, isn't she?" Joe said, waking Aven from her dreams of Heaven.

"She's amazing," Aven said, still sleepy.

"It's my bedtime. I just wanted to say goodnight. I love you, sis. See you soon."

With that, Joe climbed the stairs and headed off to his bedroom.

When Aven woke up, she knew something was wrong. It took her a moment to collect herself. What was that noise? It was like nothing she'd ever heard before. She didn't know what it was, but it felt like a knife through her heart. Suddenly everything grew dark, and she felt cold.

"Joe?" Aven called out, needing her brother. "Joe, where are you? I'm afraid. Joe, I need you."

Aven desperately searched for her beloved brother, but couldn't feel him.

Aven curled herself as tight as she could, trying to shield herself from the pain coming at her from every direction. She decided to stay like this until Joe came to save her. Until he told her everything was alright. Until she could feel his love again. But Joe never came.

Aven could feel people all around, but where there had been joy and laughter, now there was only pain and anger. She couldn't understand what was going on, and her little heart couldn't take it. Where was the love and joy she was supposed to bring? Had she somehow lost it? And where was Joe? Didn't he know she needed him? Didn't he care anymore? He said he loved her, and he had become her best friend. She couldn't make it here without him. Not before and certainly not now that all she was surrounded with was pain.

"Christos! Christos, where are You? Joe said You visit him every day. I need You! I need Joe!" Aven cried out to the darkness that was now the whole of her existence.

As soon as she cried out, a white light appeared in the distance. Aven could feel peace coming towards her.

Just then she felt a wave of grief coming from Lily. As she turned towards it, it overcame her, shielding her from the light. The darkness caved in upon her, bringing a sense of hopelessness with it.

How had this happened? How could Christos have let this happen? The pain was too much for Aven and she began to go numb. She began to give up. Nothing seemed to matter anymore. Only a few days before this, she was excited for the future.

Now, she was afraid of it.

After Joe's funeral, Celeste came to the house. Overcome with grief, Lily collapsed to the floor. Celeste ran to her sister and embraced her. As she did, Aven once again saw the white light radiating from her aunt and for a moment her pain lifted. For just a moment, she felt safe. Then, as suddenly as the light came, it disappeared.

Aven once more found herself alone, surrounded by pain and darkness.

CHAPTER 3

Delivered

THE PLACE AVEN WAS IN was becoming more and more cramped every day. She knew she couldn't stay here much longer, but fear of what was to come kept her from wanting to go anywhere. She still felt the absence of Joe every waking moment. The joy and excitement she had once felt for her future had disappeared with him. Aven's loss had been great and she missed Heaven—she missed her home. She longed to go back in time before she had agreed to this journey, before she knew pain. But she couldn't go back. She could only go forward.

With a great deal of fear in her little heart, she decided to take the next step. She couldn't stand not being able to move any longer. So, with all the courage she could muster, she stretched out, willing herself to be free of this place. Within moments, she could see light in the distance. She reached towards the light and suddenly found herself in an even tighter place. Now she couldn't move at all. "Why did I even bother?" Aven moaned to herself.

Suddenly, there was intense pressure, and then she was free. Aven stretched out, thankful to be rid of the place she'd been held captive in for so long.

Aven opened her eyes. The bright lights hurt and she tried to say something, but was shocked by the noise she heard. That couldn't be her voice. She'd never heard a noise like that before and didn't know how one would make such a racket. After taking a moment to collect herself, she tried again.

"Whaaaa!"

Aven quickly closed her mouth. That was her! "Oh, NO! Now what?!" was all she could think. Where was Joe? She needed him so badly.

She decided it was better not to try to speak, so instead she looked around. Her eyes started to adjust to this new form of light she was seeing for the first time. She was confused by what she saw or even by how she was seeing for that matter. As she looked around, she started to feel overwhelmed. Her little heart began to beat wildly. Panicked, she tried to run, but something hit her in the face. "What was that?" she wondered, looking around. Tiny arms and legs moved all around her. She tried to shield herself from them, but—"OUCH!" Something hit her in the face again. After being hit a few more times, Aven realized they were her own arms and legs. She couldn't talk, and now she couldn't even move her own arms without hitting herself. "What's next?" She was afraid of the answer to that question.

"Welcome, Aven."

Aven turned toward the familiar light. Christos!

"Christos! You're here!" Aven said as the peace His presence brought began to warm her.

"Of course I'm here, Aven. You didn't think I'd let you take this step alone, did you?" Christos said in the sweetest voice Aven had ever heard.

"I didn't know what to think," Aven responded. "I've been alone for so long. I'm tired and cold. I'm so happy my journey here is over!" Aven said, feeling the joy sweep through her.

"Oh, My sweetness, the journey has just begun. You've never been alone, though. I've been here every moment. You just haven't been able to see Me."

Aven took a moment to let the shock settle in. "This is just the beginning?" Aven asked with awe and disappointment.

"Yes, Aven, it's just the beginning. I miss you too but I know this journey will be good for you. There is still so much for you to do, to see, to enjoy here. Remember what I told you: you are a part of Me. Everything you will ever need is growing inside of you. Spending time with Me here and learning to love those around you will water those seeds. They will be ready to harvest when you are ready for them. I am always here with you even when you can't see Me. I love you more than anything. I have provided everything you need for this journey. This journey is for your benefit it's the next step in becoming one with Me. As *I AM*, so *YOU ARE*."

With that, Christos faded away. Aven had needed to hear those words. She had needed to feel Christos' love for her. Part of her still wanted to go back to Heaven, but she had a new strength. At least now she knew she was in the right place. Whatever came, Christos loved her.

Once Christos was gone, Aven once again became aware of her surroundings. Someone had wrapped her in a warm blanket and was handing her to someone who was lying in a bed.

"Hello, Nevaeh."

She knew this voice. This was her mother. Joe had told her her name was Lily. She'd wondered what her mother looked like. She was lovely. With dark curls and deep blue eyes, she had a kind face, but Nevaeh could see past that. Something dark overshadowed her mother.

As Nevaeh looked into her mother's eyes Lily smiled but Nevaeh couldn't feel her mother's joy. She only felt loneliness.

Lily held Nevaeh against her chest. They were so close Nevaeh could hear her mother's heart-beat. As Nevaeh listened to the rhythmic beat, she longed to connect to her mother. She wanted to feel her mother's love warming her little body like Christos' love did. Instead, she still felt as though she were all alone. Tired, she allowed the rhythm to carry her away into sweet sleep.

CHAPTER 4

Nevaeh's Home

A SOFT BREEZE DRIFTED over Nevaeh, waking her from her sleep.

"Heya, Aven."

A being Nevaeh didn't know flew around the room as if doing his rounds.

"Who are you?" Nevaeh asked, as peace and warmth washed over her.

"I'm Alister. You can call me Ali. I'm one of the angels assigned to you," Ali answered as though that shouldn't be news to Nevaeh.

"I have angels assigned to me?" Nevaeh asked, with both excitement and confusion.

"Um, yeah," Ali responded, not sure why this was news.

"Why? I've heard of angels interacting with humans. I remember Daniel telling me a story in Heaven about angels holding the mouth of lions closed when they tried to eat him. Paul used to tell of kinds of crazy stories about angels helping him. But why me? Why do I have angels?"

Ali laughed as he did a loop-de-loop over Nevaeh's crib. "Those were some really great times for us angels. Totally epic! But you have your own angels because you have your own missions to accomplish here on Earth."

"I have missions?" Nevaeh asked, as that concept sank in.

"Why did you think you were sent to the Realm of Earth?" Ali said still surprised that Nevaeh didn't know just how important she was.

"I mean, I knew that Christos asked me to come for a reason. Before I came He told me about my scroll and my purpose here but I hadn't thought of it as a mission."

"Reason, scroll, purpose... What's your definition of a 'mission?'" Ali asked, allowing Nevaeh to come to the correct conclusion herself.

"You're right! It is a mission. Just like Abraham had a mission. I have a mission! Ali, can you believe that I, little ol' me, has a mission?" Nevaeh was now brimming with purpose.

"Yes, I can," Ali said, tears streaming down his face he was laughing so hard. "I'm glad we're on the same page. I hear stories all the time of angels who are bored out of their minds because the human they've been assigned to doesn't get it. It's so awesome that you do. We're gonna have a blast."

Just then, Lily came into the room looking confused. She bent down and picked Nevaeh up from her crib. "What are you giggling at?" Lily asked Nevaeh, knowing she couldn't answer. Lily gave Nevaeh a bottle putting the infant back to sleep.

"Breakfast!" Lily called from the kitchen.

Nevaeh always did everything she could to please her mother, so she went into the kitchen as soon as Lily called. She wasn't sure which she preferred, being the toddler that she was now, or the infant she had been not too long ago. So much had changed, she was learning to communicate with other people now. Not that she liked communicating with people much. She still preferred talking to her angels. She still didn't feel connected to people.

Nevaeh waited for Lily to pick her up and put her in her seat. Nevaeh was certainly capable of climbing into her own chair but it didn't feel like her chair. She hated it. Everywhere she went in this house she felt like an intruder. She felt like she didn't belong and wasn't wanted. Every time she tried to touch something, she was told not to. She'd try to pick something up and someone would tell her to put it down. She had no freedom and was tired of hearing, "No!" all the time.

Deep down she knew if Joe were still here things would be different.

Breakfast did not go well and as soon as she was finished Nevaeh headed to her bedroom. She wanted to be alone. It was when she was alone that Ali came to play, sometimes even Christos showed up.

Ali was waiting for Nevaeh in her room.

"Morning Sunshine," Ali teased.

Nevaeh was in no mood to be teased. Ali's little display of affection backfired and the toddler began to cry quietly.

"What's wrong?" Ali asked concern thick in his voice.

"Why doesn't Mom love me?" Nevaeh wept in Ali's arms.

"What happened?" Ali's voice soothed.

"Mom made oatmeal again. I've told her I hate it but she keeps making me eat it." Nevaeh started to calm down as she let it off her chest.

"Maybe she thinks it's good for you," Ali reasoned, trying to make a case that Lily did indeed love Nevaeh.

"No, you don't understand. It was Joe's favorite. She makes it because she wishes I were him. She wants me to be Joe but I don't know how to be. She hates me."

Alister loved Nevaeh and wished he could reach deep down inside her and remove all her pain. But that wasn't his purpose in her life. For now, all Alister could do was hold the dear girl as she cried herself to sleep allowing the cares of the Earth Realm to fade away.

"Welcome back, Aven."

As Aven opened her eyes, delight overcame her. What a sight! She was sitting on the greenest grass she'd ever seen. It was warm and soft. Everything here was so inviting. The trees towered above her, swaying in the light breeze. The breeze, singing as it made its way through the branches. Birds chirping their song. Flowers everywhere. It was Heaven.

Aven sat there for a few minutes just letting the full scene sink in. The light was so wonderful! She could feel it soaking into her being and warming her from the inside out. All she could feel was peace and love and joy. She could sit here forever. "Coming?" the same voice called to Aven.

"In just one moment." Aven was excited for the adventure, but it had been a rough day and she needed an extra moment to adjust to the atmosphere here.

"Take your time. I could just sit here forever, too."

Aven didn't know who this being was, but she had grown to love her. She felt she could tell her anything. "What are we doing today?" Aven asked, knowing her presence meant that there was an adventure in store for her.

"What would you like to do?" The woman was smiling as she asked Aven to choose.

"Could we ride out to the ocean and go swimming with killer whales?" Aven asked, jumping to her feet, suddenly ready to go.

"Sounds like a fun adventure to me!" The woman stood up, placing the flowers that had crawled into her lap onto the grass. "Race you to the horses!" She said laughing as she starting running towards the horses waiting just a few paces away.

Aven mounted the beautiful horse that was waiting for her. Once she was settled into the saddle, they started off for the ocean.

CHAPTER 5

The Door Opens

AS NEVAEH WOKE from her dream, she lay still. Ever since she could remember, she would have vivid dreams. They were filled with color and adventure. Everything was so vibrant: she felt more alive in her dreams than in her waking hours. Lying in bed, she lingered in the peace her dreams brought her.

She couldn't help but giggle as she thought about the dream she'd just had. Dreams were wonderful—you never knew what was going to happen. Very often in her dreams she would start in the same place. It was a bank next to a softly flowing stream. There were always trees to her back and birds singing her welcome. It was always bright, always warm, and yet she never saw the sun or got too hot. The light came from a source she couldn't see and it seemed to enliven her entire being. Everything was alive. She could hear the trees whispering amongst themselves. Flowers would playfully crawl all over her when she stayed still for more than just a moment. She could interact with animals and other creatures of all kinds. She felt like a princess in her forest home.

There was also almost always a woman. She had never told Nevaeh her name, but Nevaeh felt close to her. There was something familiar about her. To Nevaeh, she seemed like she must be the most beautiful woman in the world. She had long, black, wavy hair, the greenest eyes Nevaeh had ever seen, and she was full of life. She was always up for whatever adventure Nevaeh wanted to go on. Sometimes the woman would just hold Nevaeh by the stream and tell her stories.

Best of all was Christos. It was here that Christos visited Nevaeh. Here she was free. Here she could believe whatever Christos told her. It was in this place that her heart was at peace. This place was more real to Nevaeh than anything in the Earth Realm.

Nevaeh hated waking from her dreams, for in the Earth Realm things were not so lovely for her.

"It's time!" Nevaeh heard Lily call from the other room. Nevaeh could hear her parents rushing about.

"I called your parents. They're on their way," David told Lily as Nevaeh entered the room just in time to see the twinkle in her father's hazel eyes and his wide smile showing the dimples in his cheeks. His brown hair was unusually messy. Despite his smile, Nevaeh had never seen her father look so disheveled or nervous.

"What's going on?" Nevaeh asked, wondering what all the excitement was about.

"The baby is coming," Lily beamed as she answered Nevaeh's question.

Nevaeh crawled up into her favorite chair. It was a big, overstuffed armchair that sat in the corner of their living room. From where she sat she could watch the whole scene unfold. Both her parents seemed to be in a rush, but neither one was actually doing anything. David had already grabbed a few packed suitcases from their bedroom and had them by the door. He'd also started the car and pulled it as close to the front door as possible. Now they were just standing by the door, seeming to be in a great hurry but not doing anything.

Nevaeh knew she had a baby sister coming and supposed she was due to arrive any moment. She guessed they were waiting for her by the door. She still didn't understand how the baby was coming when it was in her mother's tummy. Still, Nevaeh was happy that she'd have a little sister. She hoped that everything would be different now. She loved her baby sister and was hoping her sister would love her, too. It'd be so nice to have someone to share her life with.

"They're here! Honey, let's go," David said to Lily, putting his arm around her and helping her out the door.

"Did they forget about me?" Nevaeh wondered, watching her parents leave the house without her. They'd never left her alone before and Nevaeh didn't know what to do. Thankfully, she didn't need to figure it out as only a moment later her Grandma Matilda came through the front door.

Matilda looked young for her age. She had straight brown hair and green eyes. She'd worn it long most of her life but had recently cut it short. She was still pretty.

"Why didn't anyone tell me she was coming?" Nevaeh wondered. She loved her grandmother, but she almost never visited. It was always talked about before she came.

Too happy to dwell on the mystery, she jumped off the chair and rushed to her grandmother, wrapping her little arms around her grandma's legs.

"My sweet little thing," Matilda said, bending to pick Nevaeh up and wrap her in her arms. "I've missed you! How are you? Look at you—you're so big!" Matilda tightly embraced the little girl as Nevaeh buried her face in Matilda's neck.

Just then the door opened again. Much to Nevaeh's delight, Grandpa Bill walked in carrying a few bags. Grandpa Bill seemed like a big man to Nevaeh. He was tall, with salt and pepper hair and blue eyes. She'd seen pictures of him when he was younger and knew he'd had reddish brown hair and freckles. He was a typical Irish man and could find the humor in anything. Grandpa Bill was Nevaeh's absolute favorite.

"What are you doing here?" Nevaeh asked, as she leapt from her grandmother's arms into her grandfather's.

"We're here to watch you while your Mom and Dad are at the hospital," Matilda replied.

Bill was too busy playfully gnawing on Nevaeh's neck to answer. His beard tickled her neck, causing the young girl to roar with laughter. "What would you like to do today?" Bill asked Nevaeh as he swung the little girl around.

Nevaeh didn't even need to think about it. "Swim!" she shouted.

"Of course that's what you want to do. You're like a little fish, aren't you?" Matilda laughed, taking in the scene and delighting in Nevaeh's enthusiasm. Nevaeh had always loved the water. When Nevaeh was just a toddler, her parents had had to reinforce the gate to the swimming pool in order to keep her out.

It didn't take them long to get ready and soon they were in the backyard by the pool. It was a beautiful midsummer day. As Bill and Nevaeh splashed about in the water, Matilda sat next to the pool laughing with them. When Nevaeh's fingers looked like prunes and she'd had her fill of the water, they dried off and went inside.

The air conditioner was on inside and it felt too cold for Nevaeh, who still had wet hair. She grabbed a blanket and curled up on the couch with Grandpa Bill. Matilda put a movie in and joined them under the blanket. The little girl cuddled against her grandparents, enjoying the rare time with them.

"How long will Mom and Dad be gone?" Nevaeh asked after the movie. She wanted to meet her little sister but preferred her grandparents to her parents.

"Oh, I don't really know. Maybe never—but probably tomorrow," Grandpa Bill teased.

"It depends on when the baby comes," Matilda chimed in, rolling her eyes at Bill.

Tomorrow sounded good to Nevaeh. It meant that tonight, her grandparents were all hers.

Nevaeh woke the next morning from one of her dreams. Normally she would have stayed in bed to reflect on what she'd just dreamt about, but today wasn't just any day. Today, Nevaeh's new baby sister was coming home. She leapt out of bed, excited to see what the day would bring. She ran into the kitchen where she found her grandfather sitting at the table, sipping his coffee, and reading the newspaper. Grandma Matilda was standing over the stove.

"What'll it be, sweet thing? Eggs, pancakes, waffles? You name it and I'll make it." Matilda loved pampering the little girl on occasion.

"Anything but oatmeal," Nevaeh said happily.

Matilda looked at Bill who returned her glance with a knowing look on his face. He bent down and picked Nevaeh up. He held her on his lap, wishing her pain away.

Nevaeh's response sent a pang of pain through both her grandparents. They knew oatmeal had been Joe's favorite. They also knew that Nevaeh hated it and that Lily still made it a few times a week. They missed their grandson but loved Nevaeh. They both knew Lily loved Nevaeh, too, but that she'd found it hard to connect to her second child after the tragic death of her first.

"No oatmeal it is," Matilda smiled at Nevaeh, masking her own pain in hopes of alleviating her granddaughter's.

After a breakfast buffet consisting of pretty much everything except oatmeal, they went into the living room. "Hop up here and I'll tell you some stories," Grandpa Bill said, sitting in Nevaeh's favorite chair and patting his lap.

Nevaeh loved her grandfather's stories. He was so funny, and he always made her laugh. At his invitation, she climbed onto his lap. Lying on top of him on her stomach, she played with his beard as he told her stories. All his stories had horses in them and told of brave knights and noble kings who went on daring quests. All the princesses in the stories looked a lot like Nevaeh. She was never more content than she was sitting on her grandfather's lap.

Matilda sat close by on the couch, knitting. Upon hearing the car pull in, she got up to see if David and Lily needed any help. Knowing her little sister had finally arrived, Nevaeh turned around on her Grandfather's lap to watch the front door.

The door opened.

CHAPTER 6

Joy's Arrival

NEVAEH'S BODY TENSED as soon as she saw it. She wanted to run, to scream, to hide. She wanted to go to sleep so she could dream. But this was no dream. This was a waking nightmare.

David and Lily entered the house together. In her arms, Lily carried a little sleeping bundle. David hovered over them protectively. Nevaeh could feel the bond the three of them shared. Her parents' love for each other was stronger than ever as this new baby brought them closer together. Nevaeh could see the way her mother looked at her sister. She'd never looked at

Nevaeh that way. It was as if the new baby was the most important thing in the world to her parents. Nevaeh looked at them and saw a family. A complete family. A family she had no place in.

Nevaeh didn't move from her grandfather's lap. She couldn't move. She couldn't even cry as every ounce of hope she'd had for the new baby vanished. It was perfectly clear to her that at five years old, she'd just become an orphan. Her parents hadn't died, but in this moment, she knew they'd only ever pretended to love her. What she felt coming from them now—this was love. But it was not directed towards her.

Sensing his granddaughter tense, Bill wrapped his arms around her, holding her close. He whispered, "Babies are no fun. You're still my little girl."

Hearing Bill's voice but not what he said, Matilda turned to look at him. It was then that she, too, noticed Nevaeh's discomfort.

At Matilda's suggestion, Lily brought the baby over to Nevaeh. "Would you like to hold your new sister?" Lily asked Nevaeh, trying to include her.

Nevaeh wanted to say no, but she didn't know how to. Lily placed a pillow next to Nevaeh, who was still sitting in her grandfather's lap, and told her how to hold her arms. As Lily placed the new baby on Nevaeh's lap, Nevaeh allowed herself to hope that maybe, just maybe, she'd feel connected to her, too, and they could be a real fmily.

As Nevaeh looked at her sister whom she was now holding, love began to swell up in her. She instinctively wanted to protect her little sister. She was adorable. Nevaeh could see why everyone was swooning over her.

"Her name is Joy," Lily told Nevaeh.

And Nevaeh's heart dropped. She felt herself go cold. Joy! How could they have named her Joy? Nevaeh didn't know why, but something inside her knew that she was supposed to be the one bringing love and joy to her parents. Where had she gone wrong? And what was she supposed to do now?

Grandpa Bill tightened his arms around Nevaeh and kissed her head. He wished he could take her away and remove all her pain. He wanted to spoil the little girl, but was hardly ever even allowed to see her.

Before Nevaeh knew it, the summer was over. It was still warm, but the leaves were turning color. The pool had been closed a few weeks ago. She'd barely been able to swim since Joy arrived, anyway. What little time her parents had invested in her before Joy's birth was completely consumed by Joy now.

The only good thing that Joy's birth had brought was more frequent visits from her grandparents. Apparently, new babies were a lot of work, so Bill and Matilda had been over a few times a week to help around the house. Matilda would always swoon over Joy when she first got there, but all of Bill's time was spent with Nevaeh. Matilda would cook and clean or watch Joy so Lily could take a nap. Bill would play with Nevaeh or tell her stories.

When Bill and Matilda were there, Nevaeh didn't mind Joy—mostly because they never pushed her aside.

CHAPTER 7

The Playground

ANOTHER CHANGE the new season brought was school. Nevaeh had gone to preschool the year before and was about to start kindergarten. She didn't know how she felt about it. Part of her was happy to get out of the house for a few hours every day. She'd get to spend time with kids her own age and make new friends. But it also meant leaving Joy alone with Lily all day. That scared Nevaeh. She barely had a place in the family as it was. She was sure her mother was only too happy to be getting rid of her. At least that's what she feared.

It took Nevaeh about half a day to decide she loved school. Her teacher, Ms. Allen, was exactly what Nevaeh needed to help with the transition of being in school. She was kind and understanding.

It took Ms. Allen less than half a day to decide that Nevaeh was a favorite. The girl was bright and had a sweet disposition. Ms. Allen knew about Joe's death. Her heart had gone out to the family when it happened. Looking at Nevaeh now, she could tell the child had dealt with more pain than any child should. Ms. Allen decided then and there that Nevaeh would be her little sidekick for the year. There was something special about Nevaeh and Ms. Allen wanted to help bring it out.

At recess the first day, the kids were playing on the playground. Nevaeh noticed a little boy standing by himself with his back turned to everyone. His dirty blonde hair was a mess. Without even thinking about it, she started towards him. "Wanna play?" Nevaeh asked as she reached him.

"NO! Go away!" the little boy responded angrily.

"What's wrong?" Nevaeh asked, hearing the thickness in his voice.

"Nothing. Go away," he shouted at her.

Nevaeh was too used to rejection to let it bother her. What did bother her was not knowing what was wrong. Nevaeh stepped in front of the boy to address him full in the face. It was only then that she noticed the stain on the front of his baggy pants. The only thing holding them up was an old, worn out belt. His dark brown eyes were red and swollen.

Realizing Nevaeh knew he had peed his pants, he explained. "I was trying to hold it until we went back inside. I didn't want to make a fuss. Some of the bigger boys—" he said, pointing to a group of boys who were at least three years older— "forced me to go across the monkey bars. They blocked me so I had to just hang there. I couldn't hold it any longer. Then they made fun of me. I don't like it here. I don't like it anywhere. Please don't make fun of me or tell anyone," he begged.

"Why would I make fun of you? I promise not to tell any of the other kids, but you can't just stand here all day. We're going to go in soon and everyone will see," Nevaeh said compassionately.

"You're right." The boy started crying again.

"What's your name?" Nevaeh asked.

"Liam. What's yours?" he responded, calming a bit.

"Nevaeh. Can I go get Ms. Allen? I know she won't make fun of you and she might be able to help."

"Just promise not to tell anyone else."

"I promise."

With that, Nevaeh ran off to get Ms. Allen.

"Vay," Liam said, approaching Nevaeh the next day. "Vay... Nevaeh."

"Yes?" Nevaeh responded, waking from her daydream.

"What are you doing?" Liam asked.

"Just thinking."

"About what?"

"I don't remember," Nevaeh answered truthfully. The last thing she remembered before Liam had called her back was listening to the breeze as it blew more leaves off the trees.

"Thank you for yesterday."

"You're welcome." Nevaeh giggled, not sure what else Liam had expected her to do.

They sat talking for a few minutes. Nevaeh found herself liking Liam. She was happy she'd helped him.

"What's going on over there?" Nevaeh asked, pointing across the playground where there was a commotion. All she could see was a crowd gathered around a girl with wild, bright red hair.

"Oh, that's Sera. Courtney caught her talking to her imaginary friend just before I came over here. I guess they're all making fun of her," Liam explained.

Nevaeh paused. Images of a white being with wings who could fly and who would hold her when she cried flashed through her mind's eye. Alister. She missed Alister. It had been almost a year since her parents had explained to her that he was just her imagination. She'd held onto him as long as she could, but her parents had insisted that he wasn't real. Slowly, he had faded before disappearing completely.

"She's looney, huh?" Liam said, misreading Nevaeh's silence.

"Must be nuts," Nevaeh replied, not wanting to push Liam away. She'd already lost too many people. She couldn't afford to lose anyone else.

CHAPTER 8

Family Tree

"VAY!" LIAM CALLED, chasing after his best friend. "Wait up!"

Liam picked up his pace, almost bumping into Sera as he turned a corner. She stepped to the side just before they collided and continued walking while mumbling to herself. She hadn't even missed a beat. "She is so weird," Liam thought to himself, ignoring the girl.

Catching up to Nevaeh in the hall, he easily fell into stride with her. "What's your rush?"

"Did you hear that assignment?" Nevaeh fumed. "How could Mrs. Peterson do that to us!"

Liam didn't know how to respond. He had been close to Nevaeh for over three years and he'd never seen her this mad before. There had to be more going on. "I thought you'd enjoy it. It's kinda an art project."

"It is not an art project," Nevaeh snapped back, swinging the exit door open. School was out for the weekend and she couldn't wait to get outside.

"Is everything alright? You've been off all day." Liam was obviously concerned.

"No." Nevaeh plopped on the grass in the school courtyard under her favorite tree. She sat here often when it was warm enough. Liam dropped his book bag and sat next to her, waiting for her to vent. Looking utterly defeated, she began, "Joy's taking dance."

"Oh," was all Liam said, knowing that Joy was a sore topic for Nevaeh.

"I mean, come on. She's cute enough already and now Mom and Dad are fawning all over her. It's ridiculous. She flounces around all sweet-looking in her little pink tutu." Even as Nevaeh said it, she knew she was overreacting.

"Sounds awful," Liam teased as he saw Nevaeh relax.

"It is!" Nevaeh wasn't as upset now that she'd let it off her chest, but she was still going to give Liam a hard time about it.

"So, are you really upset about the project?" Liam wondered.

"I mean, kinda. I'm gonna need Mom's help and I hate her helping me with homework."

"At least you have a mom," Liam said, trying to help matters.

"I'm sorry, Liam," was all Nevaeh could say as she suddenly realized just how insensitive she was being.

"Don't be. Just because I don't have a mom doesn't mean that your life is perfect because you do," Liam replied sincerely.

"Who are you going to have help you?" Nevaeh asked, realizing the situation he was in and suddenly growing concerned for him.

"I don't know. Maybe Uncle Brad. He's pretty cool."

Liam lived in the same direction as Nevaeh, so they walked home together in silence.

"Mom!" Nevaeh called, dropping her jacket and bag by the front door. As much as she hated it, she knew she needed Lily's help.

"In here," Lily called from the kitchen.

Nevaeh hopped up onto a barstool at the big island in the middle of the kitchen.

"Want a snack?" Lily asked, not really sure why Nevaeh was calling her the second she got home.

"I need help." There. She'd said it. Just like pulling a Band-Aid off, she just came right out with it.

"With what?" Lily asked, realizing she couldn't remember the last time her oldest daughter had asked her for anything.

"A school project. It's due on Monday."

"What's the project about?" Lily's interest was piqued a bit.

"I need to do a family tree. I need at least three generations. I need to include aunts, uncles, cousins, and grandparents. I need to write a few sentences about everyone, showing how everyone is related," Nevaeh said, feeling mortified to be asking her mother for so much.

"Okay, how about we start after supper? It shouldn't take too long." Lily felt strange thinking about it.

"Thanks," Nevaeh said, getting up to go spend some time in her room before they ate. "Oh, and I need photos of everyone," she remembered as she was opening the door to leave.

"Okay. It will take a little longer but I'm sure we can handle it," Lily assured Nevaeh.

After supper, Nevaeh was sitting on her bed and daydreaming when a knock on the door brought her to attention. "Come in," she called. She wondered who could be knocking on her door. No one ever came in here.

"I have some pictures to go through," Lily announced, standing in the doorway. There was something about this room. Lily only went in it to clean it. It had a strange atmosphere. It felt even stranger with Nevaeh in it. "Come into the living room?" Lily suggested, feeling uncomfortable in the room.

"Okay." Nevaeh stood up and followed her mom, who was holding a shoebox full of pictures.

Making themselves comfortable on the couch—well, as comfortable as they could be in each others' presence—they opened the box.

To Nevaeh's surprise, it wasn't all that bad. As they went through the pictures, Lily told Nevaeh about the family. Most of it Nevaeh already knew, but Lily told her some stories she hadn't heard.

There was her Uncle Max. He was her mom's older brother. He was an architect who was married and had four kids. They lived about two hours away in New York City. They came up a few times a month in the summer for BBQs. He was okay. He was a little rough for Nevaeh and his kids were spoiled. He worked all the time, so he gave them whatever they wanted. It hadn't worked out very well. Nevaeh usually enjoyed seeing them, but mainly for her Aunt Samantha and their youngest daughter, Audrey. They were cool. Audrey was only a year older than Nevaeh, and they were quite a bit alike. Audrey definitely caused the least amount of drama in that family.

Then there was her Grandma Matilda and Grandpa Bill. They lived between Uncle Max in the city and Lily in the small town, but they were only about forty-five minutes from Wassaic. Nevaeh loved them! They weren't around nearly enough for Nevaeh's liking. As she went through the photos, she noticed that it looked like they used to be around a lot more. They were in most of the photos up until Nevaeh was born. She wondered what that was about.

When Lily and Nevaeh were almost through the whole box, and Nevaeh had collected the photos she was going to use for her family tree project, she froze. Chills went up and down her spine. Slowly, she reached into the box and brought out a picture of a woman—a picture of what Nevaeh thought must be the most beautiful woman in the world. She was so full of life! Of joy! Her smile looked contagious. Nevaeh knew this woman. But who was she?

"Mom, who's this?" Nevaeh asked, trembling inside.

"It's my younger sister, Celeste. I don't know how that got in there," Lily answered, taking the photo from Nevaeh.

"That's your sister? Why don't I know about her? Where is she?" Nevaeh asked.

"We don't really get along. Your Aunt Celeste is a bit of a flake."

"A flake?" This conversation was not helping Nevaeh's confusion.

"Yes, a flake," Lily replied, obviously not wanting to talk about Celeste. "She comes and goes as she pleases. Does what she wants and just flitters about from place to place as everything just seems to fall into place around her. She has no concept of reality. We aren't on speaking terms." As soon as Lily spoke so harshly, she regretted it. There had been a time when she was close to her little sister. As the memories calmed her, she turned to Nevaeh. "Why are you so interested in your Aunt Celeste?" Lily asked, as she realized her daughter was still staring at the photo Lily held in her hand.

"I dream about her almost every night," Nevaeh said so quietly Lily could barely hear her.

Not sure what to say, Lily left it at, "You've probably seen pictures of her at your grandparents'."

Nevaeh drifted off to sleep that night wondering why her Aunt Celeste was always in her dreams.

She opened her eyes and to her delight found herself in a field, next to a softly flowing stream. Flowers began crawling over Aven, tickling her arms and legs as they did. Aven laughed freely. Home!

Why couldn't this be real? Why couldn't this be her reality?

"Hi, Aven," the woman greeted her and sat down to rest next to her. As soon as she sat down, the woman could see Aven's confusion. "What's up?" she asked, genuinely interested.

"I just did a family tree for school. Mom helped me and we found a picture of you. Are you my Aunt Celeste?" Aven couldn't believe she was asking such a question of this woman—as if Aven could possibly be related to her!

"Yes, I am," Celeste answered, growing quiet. "I'm surprised I was included in a family tree your mom helped you with."

"Why?" Aven asked, more confused now than ever. How could this woman possibly be her aunt? And how could anyone possibly not just love this woman?!

"It's nothing you need to worry about. Your mom and I used to be close. One day we will be again. For now, I'm quite happy you know who I am." Celeste smiled.

"Why do I dream about you?" Aven wondered what was really going on.

"I come to you in your dreams because this is the only place I can see you. I've always wanted to be a part of your life. Here, I can be," Celeste said, rather matter-of-factly.

They sat by the stream and talked for hours.

Monday seemed to drag on forever. Nevaeh wanted school to be out for the day. She wanted to talk to Liam.

As soon as the bell rang signaling the end of the day, she grabbed her things and ordered Liam outside. Sitting under the same tree they had a few days earlier, Nevaeh didn't know where to start. But as soon as they sat, she noticed a bruise on his arm. "Are you okay?" she asked, taking his hand and choking back tears.

Liam knew it was no use trying to hide anything from Vay. She noticed things no one else did. "I'm fine. No big deal, just a fight with Dad over the family tree project. What'd you want to talk to me about?" He knew there was nothing she could do, and he wasn't ready to share everything yet. He wondered what had her so excited.

Aven wanted to tell Liam everything she'd discovered over the weekend, but before she could figure out where to start, she saw Sera watching them from across the courtyard. Sera's head was tilted as if something had piqued her interest.

"Creepy," Liam said, following Nevaeh's gaze.

"Yeah, creepy," Nevaeh responded half-heartedly.

"So, what's up?"

"Oh, uh, I have an aunt I didn't know about," Nevaeh said, reconsidering the events of the weekend. She wondered if she should tell Liam more. Nah, she thought. They're just dreams, she rationalized. But as Nevaeh stared at the empty place where she swore Sera had been just a moment before, she realized she wasn't really sure of anything anymore.

CHAPTER 9

Forest of Peace

"IT'S SO PEACEFUL HERE," Aven thought out loud. What was it about this place that did that to her? She was always thinking out loud here. It was almost as if she couldn't keep any of her thoughts to herself. Not that she minded. She knew she was safe and accepted here. It was the most wonderful feeling in the world to know you could just be yourself. No walls, no judgment, just life. It was good here.

"I agree. There is nothing like knowing you are completely accepted just the way you are. Christos was the first one who taught me that,"

Celeste chimed in, causing Aven to realize that everything she just thought had been out loud. Thinking that out loud, too, Aven and Celeste laughed together.

As they entered The Forest of Peace, they both grew quiet. There was a weightiness about this place that silenced even your thoughts. In this place, it was almost as if you ceased to exist. Everything you knew outside of this place grew dim as you were swept away into an almost dream-like state. You couldn't think, you couldn't speak: all you could do was rest as peace flooded your being, washing away all your cares and sorrows.

Celeste had first brought Aven to The Forest shortly after Aven discovered Celeste was her aunt, and now, they'd been coming here together for years. Every time Aven was feeling discouraged or wanted to give up on life, Celeste would bring her here. This time it had been Celeste who said she needed this trip to The Forest of Peace.

They always came by horseback, Celeste riding Deliverance, a big black horse she'd been given years ago, and Aven riding the colt Christos had brought her just before her first trip to The Forest. Aven loved her colt. Christos told her his name was Redemption. According to Celeste, he was a buckskin thoroughbred. All Aven knew was that he was beautiful. She had been overjoyed when she received him. She affectionately called him Demi.

They continued to wander in The Forest in silence, fully giving themselves over to the peace.

BEEP, BEEP, BEEP! Agh. Nevaeh leaned over and hit the snooze button on her alarm. "Why?!" she thought to herself. She didn't want to get up. She didn't want to go to school today. She wanted to go back to sleep, back to her dreams. She knew they were just dreams, but she didn't care. At least it was pleasant in her imagination.

Dragging herself out of bed, she reluctantly got ready for school. Coming into the hallway from her bedroom, she almost tripped over Cuddles. Cuddles was Joy's little Pomeranian. She'd gotten the dog for her fifth birthday almost a year ago. Nevaeh couldn't help but think that she hadn't gotten a puppy for her fifth birthday. Her mom had been almost nine months pregnant when Nevaeh turned five, and had been busy getting ready for Joy's birth. Just another slap in the face that told her Joy was indeed the favorite.

She grabbed an apple from the fruit bowl on the counter and headed out the front door. Liam was waiting for her at the gate.

"Morning, sunshine," Liam greeted Nevaeh, teasing her about how miserable she looked.

"It's too early for that," Nevaeh responded. "I looked it up, we're eleven years old. We should be getting eleven hours of sleep at night. How are we supposed to do that? We have too much school for that."

After their talk about how much sleep they needed the day before, he'd looked it up to. It was actually nine to eleven hours. Still, he knew better than to argue with Nevaeh this early. Give it an hour and she'd be her usual, sweet self again.

Nevaeh noticed Sera watching her as she took her seat. Why did it always seem like Sera knew when she'd had a dream?

"Do you think we should have her over?" Nevaeh overheard Lily ask David just a few minutes before dinner.

"I think it'd be rude not to. You haven't seen her for years. She's never even met the girls," David responded cautiously.

"I know."

Nevaeh couldn't make out Lily's tone. It was something close to defeat.

"She's been gone for over eleven years. Every time she's made a trip to see your parents, you've made up an excuse not to see her. But this isn't just a short trip where you can avoid her. She's been back for almost a month and has reached out to you several times. I know she hurt you, but you can't hold onto it forever. Your mom says she isn't sure what she's going to do next. What if she moves back permanently?" David reasoned, not too keen on seeing the long-lost sister-in-law but knowing how petty they'd look if they didn't.

Lily caved with mixed emotion. "You're right. Let's get the grill out this weekend and have a BBQ. If we invite the whole family, maybe I won't even need to talk to her."

At the dinner table, Lily announced that on Saturday they were having a BBQ with the whole family. "Your Aunt Celeste is back in town for a little bit and I thought it'd be nice to have her over."

Nevaeh could hear the tension in her mother's voice, but had been curious about her aunt for so long that she risked asking, "Where has she been? What has she been doing there?" She did refrain from asking why they'd never met her.

"Just a few months after I found out I was pregnant with you, Celeste went out to Texas to train a horse for show jumping. It's what she's always wanted to do, even when we were children. When the opportunity came up, she jumped on it. It was just one horse, and she was gone for a few months. The horse ended up doing extremely well. About a month after she came home, the ranch contacted her. They offered her a full-time job as their lead trainer. She was only twenty-two at the time and it was her dream job. So that's where she's been all these years," Lily explained, realizing talking about her sister didn't hurt as badly as it used to.

Nevaeh could barely sleep that night. She was going to meet her Aunt Celeste! Yet she wasn't sure she wanted to. She loved the Aunt Celeste she knew in her dreams, but they were just dreams. Who knew what she would really be like? What if the real Aunt Celeste ruined the Aunt Celeste of her dreams? She remembered her mom telling her that Aunt Celeste was "flaky" and now she found out that Celeste hurt her mom. She didn't really know what to think.

Nevaeh tossed and turned most of the night, leaving no time for dreams.

Nevaeh was a nervous wreck that Saturday. At least the whole family would be there. Even as she thought it, she realized the irony of the matter. She never fit in with the family and seldom looked forward to seeing them all at once. But perhaps today they would shield her from Aunt

Celeste and thus stop her dream world from coming crashing down around her.

"Nevaeh—they're here," Lily called, knocking on her bedroom door.

"Okay, it's time. You can do this," Nevaeh gave herself a little pep-talk before beginning the ominous journey to the backyard where her family was gathering.

Before going outside to join them, she looked out through the screen door to survey the scene. Her Uncle Max was already talking to her dad about the project he was working on at work: that's all her Uncle ever talked about. Her dad was trying to seem interested in the conversation, but was really more focused on the meat on the grill. A few of her cousins, including Audrey, were kicking a soccer ball around.

Lily was in the kitchen getting the side dishes ready with Grandma Matilda's help. Aunt Samantha was sitting outside at the patio table with Joy on her lap. Grandpa Bill was sitting at the table with her, along with a woman whose back was turned towards Nevaeh so she couldn't see her face. But Nevaeh could see the woman had long dark wavy hair. That must be Aunt Celeste, Nevaeh deducted. Other than the newcomer, it looked like any other family BBQ.

Except for Cuddles. Where was Cuddles? The dog was usually running around, barking at everyone. She didn't really care for anyone outside the immediate family and she hated strangers. Oh, well. "Good riddance!" Nevaeh thought, turning her attention from the missing dog back to the real tragedy at hand.

Nevaeh took one last breath before joining the family—one last breath to say goodbye to her dreams.

Closing her eyes and allowing herself to go numb, Nevaeh opened the back door onto the patio. Slowly, Nevaeh opened one eye. "Well, no ball of fire yet." She had thought for sure that it wouldn't take long for her life as she knew it to end. "Just give it a minute," she thought. "Hm. Still nothing."

From where she stood, Aunt Celeste seemed pretty normal. Of course, all she could see was her back. Cautiously approaching the table, Nevaeh was aware of every step she took. As she approached, she could see that Cuddles was curled up on Celeste's lap. "That's weird," Nevaeh thought. Cuddles was never calm with people around, but the dog now looked perfectly at peace.

"Hello, Nevaeh," Grandpa Bill greeted her, pulling her onto his lap. At eleven years old, Nevaeh felt silly sitting on anyone's lap—anyone but Grandpa Bill's, that is. He always felt like the life of the party to Nevaeh. He was kind of quiet and sat off to the side of the main commotion, but he was hysterical. Nothing got past him and he never passed up an opportunity to pick on someone. But he was kind and sensitive to Nevaeh, and she loved him dearly. "Nevaeh, this is your Aunt Celeste," her grandpa announced.

Aunt Celeste looked exactly how she always did in Nevaeh's dreams. Nevaeh remembered her mom telling her that she probably saw a picture of Aunt Celeste at her grandparents' house the one time Nevaeh mentioned dreaming about her. Looking at her aunt now, Nevaeh thought that must be exactly what had happened.

"Hi Nevaeh, it's nice to see you," Celeste said to Nevaeh, smiling.

"Nice to meet you too," Nevaeh replied politely.

"I just love flowers," Joy said absentmindedly, playing with the daisy she had just picked.

"Me, too," Celeste said. "Wouldn't it be fun if they were alive and could tickle you?" Celeste asked, leaning over to tickle Joy while winking at Nevaeh.

Nevaeh startled at her aunt's question. Images of flowers crawling over her and tickling her as she sat next to her aunt by a stream came flooding through her thoughts. For just a moment, it seemed as though she was in that place once again.

"Meat's done!" David called to Lily and Matilda in the kitchen, bringing Nevaeh's attention back to the BBQ. They brought out the side dishes and the family ate together.

The rest of the afternoon was pleasant enough. Celeste told the family how Robert, the man she'd been working for in Texas, had died suddenly about six weeks ago. His children had inherited the ranch and didn't have much interest in horses. They were more interested in the oil business the family owned. They were planning to sell all the horses and most of the land around the ranch house. They told Celeste she was no longer needed, and let her go. Celeste stayed for the funeral, but then had felt like it was time to come home. She wasn't really sure what she was going to do, but she felt like she was where she was supposed to be, at least for now.

Nevaeh guessed that's what her mom meant when she called Celeste "flaky." She just did what she felt she was supposed to do. Nevaeh wished she could live like that and didn't see it as being flaky. She saw it as being free. It was obvious Celeste had cared about her boss. She teared up a few times telling her story and smiled when she talked about the man. Nevaeh felt sorry for Celeste.

"Can I take a walk?" Nevaeh asked Lily, needing a break from the commotion.

"Just don't go too far," Lily said, giving Nevaeh permission to get away for a few minutes.

Nevaeh headed toward the big farm next door.

"Mind if I join you?" Celeste asked Nevaeh, falling in stride with her.

Nevaeh had wanted to be alone, but Celeste didn't feel like an intruder to her. "Okay," she simply said, continuing on her way.

They walked in silence for a little while, Celeste reflecting on her next step and Nevaeh wondering why her aunt had been winking at her all day.

"Oh, it's lovely!" Celeste said, referring to the big farmhouse they were passing.

"It's my favorite place around," Nevaeh agreed. "The people who lived there were nice. They moved about a year ago. It's been for sale ever since. They bought it when I was just little and redid it. They were planning on having horses here. They built a brand-new stable, but never used it. I've been in it: it's huge. It has like thirty stalls and a riding arena. They were going to give me lessons when they got horses, but they never did."

"I've always wanted a place like that," Celeste said as they continued to walk.

"I thought you wanted to train horses?" Nevaeh asked, wanting to know everything she could about her Aunt.

"I do," Celeste smiled, "but that's not all I want. I would love my own place. My own horses. I can't afford it, so I train other people's horses. Now that Robert is gone, I don't know what I'm going to do. I spent eleven years with those horses. I was there when some of them were born," Celeste explained.

"Oh." Nevaeh thought about that for a moment. "The people who owned this weren't rich. How much money would you need?"

"Let's just say it'd take a miracle. What I really want are horses I can train to be Olympic competitors. They can be worth anywhere from $400,000 to $15 million per horse. To do what I really want to do, I'd need about ten horses." Celeste grew quiet and stared off into the distance.

"What is it?" Nevaeh asked.

"Just a scripture the Lord keeps speaking to me over the past year or so." Celeste could tell by the look on Nevaeh's face she wanted to know more. "'*So I gave you a land that you hadn't farmed, cities to live in that you hadn't built, vineyards and olive groves that you hadn't planted. So you ate all you wanted.'* It's Joshua 24:13."

They heard Matilda calling: "Celeste, your phone is ringing!"

"Better go see what the fuss is." Celeste paused just a moment to look one more time at the beautiful house that was for sale next to Nevaeh's.

CHAPTER 10

A Land You Hadn't Farmed

"VAY. VAY!" LIAM CALLED NEVAEH, waking her from one of her daydreams. "Whatcha doing?" he asked, dropping to sit beside her under what they considered their tree.

"Thinking about Aunt Celeste." She began, "I haven't seen her since she got that call at the BBQ. I guess she left town the next day, but no one seems to know why. It's been about a month. I'm just wondering what she's up to."

"Are you worried about her?" Liam probed.

"No, I'm sure she's fine, I've just been having some weird dreams lately." Nevaeh considered telling her best friend how she'd been dreaming about her aunt her whole life. She decided it still wasn't time. What was the point, anyway? All she'd do was make him think she was nuts.

"Ready to walk home?" Liam asked, standing to start their reasonably short walk together.

"Help me up," she said, reaching her hands towards Liam. He easily pulled her to her feet and they started their walk home together.

"I can't wait for summer vacation," Liam commented. The last few weeks of school were always the hardest.

"Me either! You need to come visit me every day, though," Nevaeh told him, knowing he was planning on it. Besides, it wasn't like he wanted to spend the summer at home.

"That's the plan," Liam responded, just how Nevaeh had expected him to.

"What's going on up there?" Nevaeh wondered out loud, spotting a truck pulling out of the farm next to her house.

"Let's go see," Liam said, picking up the pace. "Looks like someone is moving into the farm next to you, Vay," Liam said as they approached the farm next to Nevaeh's house.

They decided to turn up the drive to investigate. As they did, Sera came out from behind a tree. “Hi,” she greeted them.

Liam and Nevaeh looked at each other. Of course they’d known who Sera was since the first day of kindergarten over six years ago, but neither of them had ever talked to her. Sera’s voice surprised Nevaeh. Nevaeh had always thought of the odd girl as shy, bashful, and afraid. She was always mumbling to herself and everyone thought she was looney! But the girl standing in front of them, blocking their path, didn’t seem shy or afraid. Her voice was soft, yet she spoke with confidence and looked them both right in the eye. Nevaeh knew Sera had red hair, but had never before noticed her green eyes. Sera was actually quite pretty and her presence made Nevaeh a little uncomfortable.

“What are you doing here?” Liam asked, clearly more shaken by her presence than Nevaeh was.

“I’ve been watching the activity over this place for a while now. Today things changed, and I came to investigate,” Sera told them, very sure of herself and confirming to Liam that she was crazy.

“Nevaeh lives right next door. If there’d been activity here before today, she would’ve known about it,” Liam said, basically accusing the girl of being bonkers.

"I know where Nevaeh lives. But it's the kind of activity not everyone can see," Sera said, not seeming to be at all bothered by Liam's attitude towards her. "Did you want to go look inside, or not?" she asked, as if she knew what his plan had been before running into her.

"Do you still want to, Nevaeh?" Liam asked, turning to his best friend who was standing behind him.

"Yes, let's," Nevaeh said. "You coming, Sera?" Nevaeh asked, feeling intrigued by what the girl had said about "activity." Nevaeh hadn't seen anything, but she'd been feeling movement around the place for some time.

"Yes, please. Lead the way, Vay," Sera replied, catching both her companions off guard.

"I'm the only one who calls her that," Liam spat at Sera.

"It's okay, Liam. I like the nickname you gave me. I don't mind if other people use it," Nevaeh said, not really sure why she was defending Sera, who was practically a stranger.

As they entered the stables, Sera stopped in the doorway. She looked around, tilting her head from side to side as if considering different things she was seeing.

"Weirdo!" Liam thought to himself. "Let's explore!" he said to the girls as he took the lead.

"Coming?" Nevaeh asked Sera who hadn't moved since they first entered the stable.

"I can see everything I want to from here," Sera replied.

Liam and Nevaeh looked around. From where they were standing, all they could see was the aisle. From here it was clear that the stable had just been cleaned, but that hardly told them what they wanted to know.

"Okay, then," Liam said to no one in particular. He was more convinced than ever that Sera was off her rocker and he wasn't comfortable around her. "Coming, Vay?" he directed his question to Nevaeh.

Nevaeh looked at Sera, wondering if she really could see something they couldn't. "Yup, coming." She turned to follow Liam.

"Hey, check it out. There are boxes in the office," Liam said, entering a decent sized room with a big desk that had boxes piled on top of it.

Nevaeh followed him into the room, but wasn't sure about going through someone's private property. "Do you really think you should open that?" Nevaeh asked as Liam dove into the first box.

"Don't you want to know who's moving in and what kind of horses they have? There must be that kind of info in here," Liam reasoned as he continued pawing through the boxes.

"You won't find what you're looking for," Sera said, suddenly appearing in the doorway.

Liam rolled his eyes. “What do you know?!” His tone clearly portrayed his annoyance.

“Well, I know that you won't find what you're looking for.” She paused, looking about the room, tilting her head from side to side. “And I know the horses are show horses. Jumping, I think. Yes, jumping. Hm, I've probably said too much. Well, goodbye.” With that, Sera turned and was gone.

“Okay, that was weird! Tell me you don't think she's absolutely the craziest person you've ever met?” Liam looked to Nevaeh for confirmation.

Nevaeh just shrugged. She wasn't sure why, but Sera was growing on her. There was just something about her and Nevaeh liked that she wasn't normal.

Liam continued to search through the boxes, and just as Sera had said, he didn't find any information about the new owner or the horses.

Not to be discouraged, the two children continued to explore the farm. They looked inside the stalls which had fresh sawdust spread on the new rubber mats. The tack room had been equipped with saddles, bridles, brushes, everything you'd need. Even the hayloft had been stocked with fresh hay. Whoever was coming was well-prepared.

After they had thoroughly examined the stables, paddocks, and porch of the farmhouse,

Nevaeh was so excited that after saying goodbye to Liam, she ran the whole way home.

Not even stopping long enough to wonder whose new black Cadillac was sitting in the driveway, Nevaeh burst through the front door and instantly stopped in her tracks.

Lily was sitting on the couch. Nevaeh knew her mom and knew this was how she looked when she was trying to be polite but was not happy about something. The overstuffed recliner slowly turned around to reveal the source of Lily's displeasure.

"Nevaeh!" Celeste greeted her niece, brimming with pleasure. "How are you? Are you excited for the summer?" Celeste asked.

"Aunt Celeste! What are you doing here?" Nevaeh asked, both surprised and happy to see her aunt.

"She's moving in," Lily said in a sharper tone than she had intended. Immediately, she regretted saying anything. "I'll go get some drinks and snacks. Nevaeh, keep your aunt company," Lily said as she headed for the kitchen.

"You're what?" Nevaeh wasn't sure how Aunt Celeste was going to move in when Lily clearly didn't want her to.

"Moving in. Well, next door," Celeste explained to the confused child.

"You're the one who bought the farm?" Nevaeh beamed.

"Sure am!" Celeste said, tears coming to her eyes.

"But how? You said it'd take a miracle for you to be able to do something like that!" Nevaeh was desperate to know more. She was desperate to believe in miracles—desperate to believe that dreams could come true.

"It's a long story," Celeste said as Lily came back into the room carrying a tray with tea and lemonade, as well as a plate of cheese, fruit, and crackers.

Lily settled herself onto the couch. She patted the seat next to her, bidding Nevaeh to sit. Putting her arm around her daughter, she looked at her sister. "So, tell it. We have time."

Nevaeh couldn't remember one other time that her mother had put her arm around her like this. She wasn't sure if it was for her benefit or her mom's. But she wanted to hear the story, so she turned to her aunt, ready to listen.

Celeste began. "Remember the phone call I got last time I was here?" She waited for them to nod their response. "It was Robert's lawyer, Mr. Kinney. He told me that I was needed back in Texas. A letter Robert wrote had been found and it concerned me. I didn't really think much of it.

I thought maybe Robert had left me a few thousand dollars, knowing his kids would let me go. He was a kind man and would've wanted to help me in any way that he could.

"Anyway, Mr. Kinney said there was a plane ticket in my name and I was needed as soon as possible.

"The will had been read weeks before this and Robert left the oil business, most of his money, and the ranch to his kids. That's exactly what I had expected him to do and I didn't really know why I was needed at this point."

Celeste paused, collecting herself. "A few weeks after I came home, Mr. Kinney found a letter from Robert. He knew his kids didn't want anything to do with the horses and would sell them after he passed. He wrote that he couldn't take the thought of me being torn from the horses I'd worked so hard with and loved so much. He also wanted to make sure the horses were well-taken care of. So, he left me all the horses.

"Apparently, the family had known about the letter and tried to hide it. They didn't want the horses. But when they tried to sell them, they couldn't because Robert had me listed as co-owner of all of them. Before they could sell the horses they had to prove that they were the legal owners. They probably would have succeeded if Mr. Kinney hadn't found the letter."

Celeste was crying by this point. “I sold a few of them. They were worth a lot of money. I made more than enough on the ones I sold to buy the farm next door. I was able to keep the horses I was closest to.” Now, as tears ran down her face, Celeste began laughing.

Nevaeh noticed that Lily was crying, too.

“When do you move in?” Nevaeh asked.

“My things are being moved in over the next few days. The horses arrive next Saturday,” Celeste beamed.

Nevaeh wasn't sure what to say. She couldn't believe what she was hearing. Only a month ago, Celeste said it would take a miracle. Nevaeh was excited for there to be horses next door and for some reason felt close to her aunt. She wondered if her mom sensed it, too, because Lily tightened her arms around Nevaeh and said, “Congratulations. I guess you got everything you've always wanted.”

Later that night, Nevaeh lay in bed thinking about the day. Why did Robert leave Celeste the horses? Was it just out of the kindness of his heart or was there more going on behind the scenes? At the BBQ, her aunt had told her the Lord had been giving her a scripture. She remembered the scripture. She had looked it up after her aunt left suddenly. Nevaeh's family didn't go to church or even talk about God, but Grandma Matilda had given her a Bible for her tenth birthday.

The scripture was Joshua 24:13. "*So I gave you a land that you hadn't farmed, cities to live in that you hadn't built...*" Isn't that exactly what had just happened to her aunt? Years before now, people had redone the farmhouse, built stables, installed fences. After being there today, Nevaeh knew that it had everything her aunt would need to train Olympic-quality horses. And the people had never even used it. They moved before buying a single horse.

And what was with Sera? Had she really been seeing something? Had she really known that Liam wouldn't find anything? Was it just a good guess about the horses?

As Nevaeh finally drifted off to sleep, she thought she saw a white being standing above her protectively, and a very familiar sweet voice saying, "All things are possible, Nevaeh."

CHAPTER 11

Hopes and Dreams

THE FOLLOWING SATURDAY couldn't come quickly enough for Nevaeh. Her days seemed to drag on. All she could think about was the excitement surrounding the neighboring farm.

When the day finally arrived, Nevaeh woke to the sound of big trucks. She leapt out of bed, threw her clothes on, yelled to her mom that she would be next door, and ran out the front of the house. She couldn't wait to see the horses.

There was a line of trucks waiting their turn to drive up the driveway and unload their cargo at the stables. Nevaeh had never been around trucks this big and decided she'd cut through the woods in her side yard, just to be safe. Coming out of the trees on the other side, she saw Aunt Celeste standing in the yard under a big oak tree close to the stables. A truck was just pulling down the driveway to leave. As it pulled into the road, Celeste saw Nevaeh.

"Hey, sweetie!" Celeste called to Nevaeh. "Come on over."

"Is it safe?" Nevaeh asked, a little intimidated by the big trucks.

"Of course it's safe," Celeste called back. "It's going to take the next truck a few minutes to back in. Come here."

Still a little unsure, Nevaeh slowly walked up to the driveway. Then, looking both ways, she ran across it as fast as she could.

"Nice of you to join me," Celeste gently teased her niece.

"The noise woke me up. How many horses are here?" she asked excitedly.

"Two are already in their stalls. About a dozen more still need to be unloaded," Celeste told Nevaeh.

"They're settling in nicely," Sera said, joining them under the tree.

"What are you doing here?" Nevaeh asked Sera. They were on speaking terms now, but Nevaeh still wouldn't really call Sera a friend.

"I saw the activity. I was curious. Is it okay that I'm here, Celestial?" Sera asked Celeste.

"Of course, Seraphina. I thought you might show up today," Celeste replied lightheartedly.

"Celestial? Seraphina?" Nevaeh wasn't really sure what was going on or who to address the question to.

"Celestial is my full name," Celeste told Nevaeh. "Celeste is just a bit shorter and easier to say."

"Seraphina is my full name," Sera chimed in. "Not many people call me that, though."

Nevaeh was about to ask how they knew that about each other when she did not, but just before she asked, a trailer pulled up. Overcome with excitement, Nevaeh turned her attention towards it.

"Howdy, Celeste," said a big man wearing faded jeans and a flannel shirt while tipping his big-brimmed hat as he approached the three girls.

"Tom!" Celeste greeted him, throwing her arms around the big man. "Tom, this is my niece, Vay, and a good friend of ours, Sera. Girls, this is Tom. He used to manage the ranch for Robert."

"Ladies," Tom said, smiling at the girls. "How are things going here?" Tom asked Celeste.

"Well, I'm about settled into the house. The barn's been set up for a week. Just need to get all the horses settled in." Celeste was beaming as she talked about her newly acquired life.

"Okay, well, let me get this big boy into his stall and move the truck out of the way. I'll be back in just a few minutes to catch up." Tom walked over to the trailer, opened the door, and disappeared inside. A few moments later he reappeared with the biggest, blackest horse Nevaeh had ever seen. Well, in real life, that is.

Celeste walked up to the stallion. "Hey Big D. How's my boy?" she asked as the horse placed his forehead against hers. The big horse closed his eyes and stood perfectly still, seeming to relax at Celeste's touch. "He's the big stall on the end," Celeste told Tom, releasing the horse's face and coming back to stand with the girls.

A few minutes later, Tom had Big D settled in his stall, the truck moved, and now he stood with the girls in the shade.

"So, what's your plan?" Tom asked Celeste as they waited for the next trailer. He was really hoping she had one.

"Well, you know about Robert leaving me the horses. The Gold Ranch in France has been interested in High Waters and Prancing Prince for a few years. As you know, Robert had no intention of showing at an Olympic level. No one could touch High Waters and Prancing Prince at the level he was showing them, but Gold Ranch thinks they have Olympic potential. They have a world-class facility and some of the best trainers in the world. When they heard I'd inherited the horses, they contacted me. I trained them, so if they do well at an international level, my name gets out there. So, after praying about it, I sold them. A few other ranches contacted me about other horses. I sold a few which gave me enough money to make a really nice start here.

"I felt like I was supposed to keep the horses that are coming today. I can see myself training them and taking on a few boarders. Not a ton, just ten or so—you know, enough to cover my monthly expenses. I'll give lessons, do some outside training for other people, and trust that I'll be successful," Celeste finished with a laugh.

"I'd like to stay for a while and help you get established, but I need to get home to Sally and the kids." There was a concern in Tom's voice.

"I know you do. Don't worry about me, I know this is a God-thing. There's no way I'd be here right now without Him. I have faith that it's gonna be great. It's just a side to the business I know nothing about. But hey, 'If you know what you're doing, you aren't learning anything.' Right?!" Celeste elbowed Tom as she said it. The older man did not look amused. "Oh, come on," Celeste tried to assure him. "Besides, a few of the ranches I sold horses to have been in the business for years. They know my situation and said if I need anything they'd be happy to help me. So, I do have people I can go to if I need advice."

"Well, I'm one of them," Tom said, clearly not convinced Celeste knew what she was getting herself into.

Nevaeh listened to the conversation her aunt was having with Tom. She loved hearing her aunt talk. It was funny to her. It was clear that her aunt didn't really know what she was doing, but that didn't seem to bother her at all. She just had faith it was not only going to work out, but that it would be great.

Where did she get her confidence, Nevaeh wondered. The conversation had given Nevaeh a better idea of why her mom considered her little sister "flaky." Nevaeh, on the other hand, was becoming more and more convinced this was the only way to live. After all, Aunt Celeste was living her dream. She hadn't made it to the Olympics yet, but some of the horses she'd trained were heading there and besides, her dream was to *train* Olympic champions, not to *be* one. At least Celeste had a dream. Most of the adults Nevaeh knew did not.

"Oh, it's beautiful!" Sera said, watching a gray horse with red mane walk out of the last trailer. "What's its name?" she asked Celeste.

"This is Ember's Flame," Celeste said, nudging Sera and leading the girls over to meet her. "She doesn't like jumping much, but boy does she have flare. She's a sweetheart, too. I'm not sure what I'm going to do with her yet. I'm not going to force her to jump when she doesn't want to, and she's a bit young to use as a lesson-horse. She doesn't really fit into my vision, but I haven't felt like I can part with her yet. I just haven't found the right person to sell her to, I suppose." Celeste smiled at Sera. It was the kind of smile that said Celeste was up to something.

Nevaeh stood back a bit as Ember was led into the stables. There were so many horses, she didn't know which was her favorite.

Celeste pulled the girl from her thoughts when she asked, "School lets out for the summer next week, doesn't it, Nevaeh?"

"Yes, we have half-days all this week and Thursday is our last day for the year," Nevaeh said, clearly thankful that that was the case.

"Good. If your afternoons are free, you can come over and spend some time with the horses. They'll be nice and settled by next Friday, and I can start giving you lessons then," Celeste said to Nevaeh.

"Can I take lessons, too?" Sera asked Celeste.

"That, dearie, is a question for your parents. Before you leave I'll give you my number and you can have them call me," Celeste promised Sera.

"Well, I'd love to stick around, but the horses are all settled and I have a long drive back to

Texas," Tom said as he embraced Celeste. "Remember, me and Sally are just a call away. If you run into something you can't handle, we'll do what we can."

"Thanks, Tom. Tell Sally I love her," Celeste said, patting the big man on the back.

"Who's gonna take care of all the horses?" Nevaeh asked, watching Tom's truck pull away.

"I hired a few hands. Some of the guys you saw here today work for me. They live here and flew out to Texas last week to help transport the horses. Jim, the biggest guy, he had dark hair and light brown eyes. He was the one wearing the purple shirt?" Celeste waited for the girls to acknowledge they knew who she talking about. "He's my new right-hand man around here. He'll be staying in the apartment above the stables. You girls will like him. I've told him who you both are and he knows you're both welcome here anytime. Just no riding without me and don't go into the stalls unless Jim or I are around. Okay? Someone will always be around, so make sure to tell whoever is here what you're doing. Some of the horses are pretty high-strung and I don't want either of you getting hurt. Understood?" Celeste waited until both girls had agreed to her terms.

Nevaeh was so excited she would have agreed to just about anything.

“Okay.” Celeste continued, “Now that that’s out of the way, let’s go check out the stables.”

“I really need to get home. It’s past my lunchtime,” Sera informed them.

“Okay, here’s my number. Have your mom or dad give me a call.” Celeste handed Sera a card.

Sera turned and skipped down the driveway, throwing Nevaeh a wink as she went.

“I guess it’s just us, kiddo,” Celeste said as she started for the stables. “Coming, Aven?” Celeste winked at Nevaeh.

Aven! Nevaeh froze. Why had her aunt just called her that? Where had she heard that name? That was Nevaeh’s name in all her dreams, but no one knew that. She’d never told a soul. Nevaeh had chills all over her body. Something told her that her life was about to change.

“Coming?” Celeste called again from the entrance to the stable.

Nevaeh shook off the feeling. She must have been hearing things. She probably shouldn’t have skipped breakfast. “Coming,” she called back, racing to the doorway.

They entered the stables together. It smelled like fresh sawdust, hay, and horses. This was a new smell to Nevaeh, but she found it incredibly comforting. As her eyes began to adjust to the dimmer light, she looked around. She'd seen most of the horses as they were unloaded from the trailers, but seeing the stalls full of horses sent a wave of delight through Nevaeh.

"Where's Big D?" Nevaeh asked, wanting a closer look at him. He looked very similar to the horse Celeste rode in Nevaeh's dreams.

"He's at the other end. His stall is between the tack room and the door to the arena," Celeste answered.

Nevaeh began walking down the aisle, looking at the horses as she passed them. They were all so beautiful. As she neared the middle of the barn, she noticed a big bow on one of the stalls. Celeste was right behind Nevaeh and sensing her niece had finally noticed the bow—a big red bow Celeste had chosen on purpose, hoping it would catch her niece's attention—she said, "There's someone here I think you know."

Shivers went up and down Nevaeh's spine as Celeste said it, and she turned to her aunt. Celeste nodded her head, telling Nevaeh it was alright. "Go ahead," was all she said.

Nevaeh walked to the stall and read the name on the door: "Redemption." Nevaeh couldn't breathe. The room was spinning. "What is happening right now?" was all she could think. She turned to her aunt, needing direction.

"It's alright. You can look," Celeste assured her.

Nevaeh didn't want to look. Terror had overcome her. Redemption was the name of the horse Christos had given her in her dreams. She knew the horse she affectionately called "Demi." What if this was really that horse? What would it mean? What if it wasn't? She wanted it to be so badly. She wanted to believe that her dreams were real.

Suddenly, she was swept back to a time when she did believe, a time when her dreams were more real to her than reality. She wanted it to be true; she wanted to believe again. "Oh, dear God, please," she thought as she nervously approached the stall. Her hand was shaking as she grabbed the wooden door to pull herself up onto her tiptoes. Slowly, she peeked in.

Standing before her was a beautiful buckskin colt. Demi neighed a greeting as he lifted his head over the door and nuzzled Nevaeh.

Something inside Nevaeh, something deep, deep inside Nevaeh broke. Celeste rushed to the precious girl and held her. Nevaeh stood there weeping hysterically in her aunt's arms as her new colt continued to nuzzle her.

"It was real. It was really real," was all Nevaeh could get out.

"Of course it was real, Aven. Heaven is more real than anything in the Earth Realm." Celeste smoothed Nevaeh's hair. "Let it out, let it all out."

That's exactly what Nevaeh did. As she stood there she let go of all her doubt, all her pain, and for the first time in a long time, she gave herself over to her hopes and dreams.

CHAPTER 12

Accepted

UNDER HER FAVORITE TREE in the school courtyard, Nevaeh sat with her eyes closed. She listened to the soft breeze swirling around her. Peace had been her constant companion since the previous Saturday. Her dreams were alive again. She'd never stopped having dreams, but since Saturday she'd stopped dismissing them as just dreams. Since Saturday, it seemed to Nevaeh that anything was possible. She took a deep breath as another wave of peace swept over her.

"Vay," Liam said, joining Nevaeh under the tree.

"Hi, Liam," Nevaeh smiled at her friend.

"You okay?" Liam asked, searching his friend's face for a reaction.

"I'm great," Nevaeh responded with a smile.

"You've been acting funny all day. If you're okay, what's up?" Liam was intrigued. Nevaeh seemed different, somehow.

Years ago, Nevaeh had almost told Liam how she dreamt about her Aunt Celeste before she had ever met her. She'd also wanted to tell him about Alister on their second day of school when the kids were picking on Sera for talking to her invisible friend. Fear had always held her back. Liam was always outspoken about not believing in anything like that, so she'd held back. Nevaeh hadn't wanted to lose him, so she'd gone along with him. She still didn't want to lose her best friend, but she knew it was time to tell him everything. She didn't know how she knew, she just knew. She laughed to herself as she wondered if that's how Celeste felt all the time.

Taking a deep breath, Nevaeh began, "I need to tell you something."

"You know you can tell me anything, Vay. I'm your best friend. I'll always be here for you." Liam couldn't imagine anything Nevaeh could possibly tell him that would upset him. Of course, Liam had always done his best to dull his imagination.

"I've been having dreams my whole life, and it turns out they were real," Nevaeh burst out. She knew it wouldn't go over well, but it felt so good to include Liam in her craziness.

"What are you talking about?" Liam was thoroughly confused by Nevaeh's outburst.

"I've wanted to tell you so many things over the years, but I was afraid you'd stop being my friend. Remember that day on the playground when everyone was picking on Sera?"

"Which time?" Sera was always being picked on. Liam had no idea which time Nevaeh was referring to.

"The first time. The time when Courtney had overheard Sera talking to her imaginary friend." Nevaeh remembered it all too well and now regretted not befriending Sera at the time.

"Oh, the first time. Yeah... I sorta remember," Liam understated. The fact was that he remembered that day in vivid detail, from the blue jacket Sera had been wearing right down to the fact that Sera looked more confused by the kids picking on her than she looked scared or hurt.

"Okay: I don't think it was her imagination." Nevaeh paused, waiting to see Liam's reaction.

He didn't say anything, but he didn't look amused.

Nevaeh hesitated for just a moment, then plowed on. "I think Sera sees into the spiritual realm. I used to, too. I had a friend Alister. He used to come play with me all the time. He was an angel, and I know he was real. I knew it at the time, but my parents told me it was just my imagination. I held onto him for as long as I could, but I ended up believing my parents instead of myself."

"Nevaeh, you sound crazy," Liam said as he stood up.

"Liam, wait—" Nevaeh pleaded.

"I don't want to hear it. There is no such thing as a spiritual realm. Angels aren't real, demons aren't real. You've lost your mind!" Liam shouted just before running away from her.

Nevaeh didn't move from under the tree. She wanted to go after him, but what was the point? She'd known this was how he would react.

"He'll come around," Sera said, suddenly standing close to Nevaeh.

"How do you know?" Nevaeh asked, not prepared for Sera's answer.

"I've been to the future. So, I know how he turns out," Sera stated, as though that was a perfectly normal explanation.

"I'm sorry—you've been where?" Nevaeh asked, sure she'd misheard the girl... *hoping* she'd misheard the girl.

"The future," Sera said again, not seeming at all bothered by the look on Nevaeh's face.

"Oh, I didn't hear you the first time," Nevaeh lied. In some ways, it wasn't a lie: Nevaeh had heard what Sera said, but she couldn't really *hear* what Sera was saying. Nevertheless, just five minutes prior Sera had become Nevaeh's closest friend. So, not having anyone else to turn to, Nevaeh just went with it.

"We should get going to the farm. Celestial will be waiting for us," Sera said, offering Nevaeh a hand to help her to her feet.

"Thanks," Nevaeh said, taking Sera's hand.

Then Nevaeh asked Sera the question she'd been wanting to ask for some time: "Why doesn't it bother you when people pick on you?"

"Why would it bother me?" Sera responded, not at all put off.

"Don't you want people to like you?" Nevaeh pushed the matter.

"I suppose if I got to choose, it'd be nice if people liked me, but just because they don't like me doesn't mean I don't like them. What does it really matter if they like me or not?"

"I don't know. I can't explain it. But don't you want to be accepted?" Nevaeh reasoned.

"I am," Sera said, looking a bit confused by Nevaeh's perspective.

"Who accepts you?" Nevaeh hoped she wasn't hurting Sera. "You don't have any friends at school."

"You're my friend," Sera pointed out.

"Yes, I am," Nevaeh said, surprised that hearing Sera call her a friend made her feel somehow more whole. "But I'm your only friend. Everyone else thinks you're crazy." Nevaeh assumed Sera knew that.

"I know," Sera laughed. "But why do I care what other people think? If you had a good friend but they went to another school, would you stop believing they existed just because no one else knew them or believed they were real?"

"No!" Nevaeh laughed at the thought. "Why would I care? If they were my friend I'd stand by them."

"Exactly," Sera pointed out. "Just because no one else can see my friends doesn't mean they don't exist. I have lots of angels around and I'm friends with a lot of people in the Great Cloud of Witnesses. I don't care that no one believes me. It doesn't make them any less real."

Nevaeh wasn't sure about half of what Sera had just said, but she knew Sera was right. Who was she or anyone else to judge?

The two girls walked beside each other in silence. Nevaeh was lost in her thoughts about Liam and what Sera had just said. Sera—well, who really knows where Sera was? The possibilities were endless.

"Little ladies!" Jim called out, approaching the girls as they entered the barn. The girls had only seen him briefly on Saturday, but just as Celeste had predicted, they adored him right away. He was tall with big broad shoulders, short dark hair, and light brown eyes. He was extremely polite and had a good sense of humor.

"Good afternoon, sir," Nevaeh said politely.

"None of that, you hear?! It's 'Jim' to you both," Jim instructed them, smiling a big white toothy smile. "Celeste had some errands to run. She asked me to help you girls put horses in the crossties and teach you how to groom them."

"What are crossties?" Nevaeh asked.

"Oh, boy. We've got our work cut out for us," Jim teased as he led them first to Demi's stall. He showed the girls how to put a halter on him, clipped his lead to the halter, and walked him out of his stall into the middle of the aisle where there was a rope on either side. He took the rope from both sides of the aisle and clipped them to the halter. "This, ladies, is how you put a horse in crossties."

"Oh, that makes sense," Nevaeh said.

"Sera, Celeste said you could groom Ember." Jim led Sera to the beautiful gray mare's stall.

Every afternoon that week was spent very much the same. The girls learned how to groom and feed the horses. Jim even had them both cleaning out stalls. It was hard work for the small girls, but neither of them complained. They were both completely in love with the horses.

"Nevaeh?" Liam cautiously approached Nevaeh on the last day of school. He hadn't spoken to her all week, and he missed her.

"Liam," Nevaeh said, surprised to hear him address her.

"I'm sorry, Vay. I didn't mean to be mean to you. I just love you and don't want to see you get hurt," Liam apologized, sincerely needing her to understand.

"I missed you," Nevaeh told him, wondering what he meant when he said he didn't want to see her get hurt.

"Still friends?" Liam asked, hoping she really had missed him.

"I'll always be your friend," Nevaeh assured him.

Things felt different with him now, but he'd always been her best friend, and she loved him.

CHAPTER 13

Fear and Fire

"IS NEVAEH IN, PLEASE?" Sera asked Lily, as Lily opened the door for her on Friday morning.

"Come in," Lily told Sera. "Nevaeh, you have someone here to see you," she called to Nevaeh who was in her room getting ready for her first riding lesson.

"Sera—Hi! What are you doing here?" Nevaeh asked as she came down into the living room where Sera was sitting in Nevaeh's favorite chair, waiting for her.

"I thought you might need help with your hair," Sera answered, not moving from where she was sitting.

"I was just going to put it in a ponytail." Nevaeh thought the idea of needing help with her hair was a bit silly.

"If you do that, the helmet won't fit." Sera pointed it out in a way that didn't make Nevaeh feel stupid.

"Oh, I hadn't thought of that," Nevaeh said, laughing at herself.

"That's okay. I did," Sera said, jumping to her feet. "I brought hairnets."

"Thanks, Sera. Here, come in my room and you can help me." Nevaeh turned to lead the way.

As they entered Nevaeh's bedroom, Sera stopped in the doorway. After surveying the room for a moment, she smiled and stepped in. "Let's get you ready to ride."

Nevaeh sat at her dressing table and watched Sera do her hair.

"See? Easy," Sera said as she finished. "You can keep the hairnets so you can do it yourself next time."

"That does look easy." Nevaeh smiled at herself in the mirror. She looked funny with hairnets on. "Thanks again."

"Of course. Anytime." Sera smiled at her new friend. "It's time to head over."

"Be careful! Riding is dangerous," Lily called to the girls as they skipped out the front door. She wished she could stop Nevaeh from riding, but she and David had discussed it. He had made some excellent points. While Lily still didn't like the idea of Nevaeh riding, she saw David's points and knew how much it meant to Nevaeh. So, she had conceded to their wishes.

Giggling with excitement, the two girls bounced over to the neighboring farm. Jim was in the stables waiting for them.

"Good morning, girls," Jim greeted them as they joined him next to Ember. "Demi is all tacked up and already in the arena with Celeste. Let me just get the bridle on Ember and we'll go in together."

The girls waited anxiously for Jim to lead them in.

"Hi, girls," Celeste called as they entered the arena. Nevaeh hadn't been in the arena before today. She'd peeked in the day she had been exploring with Liam and Sera, but she hadn't realized how big it was until just now.

"Nevaeh, come on over and we'll get you mounted," Celeste instructed.

Nevaeh felt nervous at the thought of riding for the first time. It seemed a little silly to her because she'd been around horses and looking forward to riding all week. She loved Demi and knew he'd be gentle with her.

"Nevaeh?" Celeste woke Nevaeh from her thoughts.

Nevaeh realized she'd stopped about halfway to Celeste. "Oh, coming," she said as she covered the distance between them.

"Okay, if you want to climb the mounting block, I'll line Demi up." Celeste brought Demi around the mounting block directly in front of Nevaeh. "What you want to do is hold the reins and Demi's mane in your left hand. Good. Now grab the back of the saddle with your right hand. Just like that. Put your left foot in the stirrup, pull yourself up and swing your right leg over the saddle while bringing your right hand to your left hand."

Nevaeh didn't move. She stood there holding the reins and mane in her left hand and the back of the saddle with her right hand, but she couldn't move. She didn't know why, but she was terrified. Every muscle was refusing to cooperate and she was stuck there, frozen in fear.

"Vay?" she heard Liam call from behind her. His voice snapped her out of the trance she had been in. "Vay, you okay?" Liam asked. "I knew you were taking your first lesson today and wanted to come support you."

"No. I'm not okay." Nevaeh began to cry.

"Okay, sweetie. Just breathe," Celeste said, putting her arm around Nevaeh. "Tell us what's wrong."

"I'm scared." Nevaeh sobbed. "Why am I so scared?" she asked, shaking.

"It's okay, hun. I used to be afraid to ride, too. I know just what to do," Celeste assured her niece.

"You do?" The information her Aunt had just given her calmed Nevaeh some.

"Yes, I do. I'd actually forgotten all about it. It was so long ago. But yes—I know what to do. Jim, could you please take care of the horses?"

"You're the boss." Jim winked at Celeste and took Demi's reins from her.

"Come on, kids," Celeste said to Nevaeh, Sera, and Liam. "I think you're old enough to know about this stuff."

The three eleven-year-olds followed Celeste out of the stables and into her backyard. She walked a little ways and settled under a big weeping willow. The children followed her lead and sat around Celeste in the shade.

"What are we doing?" Nevaeh asked, wondering what this had to do with her fear.

"We are going to change your DNA." Celeste smirked as she said it.

"What?!" Liam and Nevaeh exclaimed in unison. Sera just smiled.

"It will be much easier to show you than to explain it to you. Nevaeh, something happened a long time ago to one of our ancestors. It was a traumatic experience and fear entered his DNA. He passed that particular fear down the family line through DNA. We are going to go to Heaven to ask Christos to remove that fear from you. I don't know exactly what will happen. We'll just follow Christos and trust Him."

"Can you really do that?" Nevaeh asked, amazed.

"Of course. That's what I did when I realized I was afraid to ride."

"Okay, then let's do this," Nevaeh said, not sure she believed it would work, but intrigued enough to give it a try.

"A few ground rules. You need to know that the only safe way to travel into a different realm is through the Blood of Christos. He is the only safe door. There are many doors to this realm, but Christos is the only safe one." Celeste reached out to hold Liam's hand. "All we are going to do today is ask Christos to come and show us how to free Nevaeh from her fear. We're only going to go where He leads us." Celeste looked around at the faces of those gathered under her tree. "Ready?"

"Ready!" Sera was the first to speak.

Nevaeh nodded, not sure exactly what to expect.

Liam wasn't sure he was ready, but he couldn't move. It felt like something inside of him was waking up. He didn't know what it was and didn't believe anything he was hearing, but still he couldn't shake the feeling.

Celeste closed her eyes. "Christos, Nevaeh is afraid. We ask You to come and show her how to conquer that fear."

The world around Nevaeh faded away.

Nevaeh found herself standing in the forest by the stream she knew so well from her dreams.

"Welcome, Aven."

Aven turned to see a massive lion standing before her.

"I'm so happy you've come today. I've been waiting for you a long time," the lion spoke in a voice she knew. It was the sweetest voice she'd ever heard.

"Christos?" Aven asked.

"Yes, Aven. I take many forms. Today, I am The Lion because you will need a lion's courage to face the fears you have asked Me to help you with. Are you ready?" Christos asked, rubbing His face against hers. He was so close she could feel His breath.

"I will go where You lead," Aven said, knowing she could trust Christos.

Christos turned and stood next to Aven. He shook His mane and roared into the ground. It only took a moment for Aven to find herself in a place she'd never been.

Feeling someone take her hand, Aven turned to her right. Seraphina was standing there next to her, her red hair wild in the wind. Aven asked Seraphina, "What's going on?"

"We traveled back in time," Seraphina told Aven.

"We *what*?" Aven asked.

"The Heavenly Realm is outside of time, so when we're in Heaven time doesn't exist. It doesn't really exist in the Earth Realm either, but I don't think you're ready for that one yet."

Aven was about to ask her to explain, but her thoughts were interrupted.

"Look!" Seraphina commanded as her green eyes turned a shade of blue Aven had never seen.

As Aven looked, the landscape changed. She was standing by an old farmhouse. There was a split-rail fence to the side of the house. It looked like they were on a farm sometime during the 1800's. A little boy walked out of the house towards the fence. He called out, and suddenly a big brown horse appeared. The boy put a bridle on the horse and climbed onto his back. They took off at a gallop. Aven watched the whole scene unfold. It was like she was right next to the boy.

The boy and his horse rode carefree through the field, but suddenly the horse tripped. He fell to his side on the hard ground. The boy's leg was caught under the horse as the horse struggled to get to his feet. Something was clearly wrong. The horse couldn't stand and the boy was trapped under him. The boy tried to calm the panicked horse to no avail.

A man carrying a gun rushed towards them from across the field. The man yelled to the boy, "What's going on?!"

"He tripped," the boy wept.

"How many times have I told you he's not for riding? He's a work horse. We need him to plow the fields." The man was furious at the young boy.

"I'm sorry," the boy begged for forgiveness, but the man wasn't listening.

"You broke his leg," the man spat, hitting the boy. "Now we have no horse to plow the fields. If the family starves to death, it's on you."

The boy accepted that the fate of the family was on his shoulders. But the weight of the responsibility was too much for the small child, and it opened a door. Fear quickly grasped the opportunity.

As Aven watched, she saw a black figure enter the boy and fear overcame him. The man used a log to lift the horse off the boy's leg, allowing him to escape. But the damage had been done.

Aven wept as she watched. She could feel Fear inside her and knew that this was where that fear had come from. A voice—she didn't know exactly where it came from—but a voice deep inside her cried out, "Forgive me... I repent of my fear. I repent for allowing Fear to control me. Fear: GO, in Christos' name!"

As soon as she was done speaking, a black figure stepped out from inside Aven. Aven fell to the ground as the weight of her fear lifted. She bowed her head to say a prayer of thanks.

"Let there be FIREEEEE!"

Aven turned to the voice. Seraphina burst into holy flames and two fire beings swept down from behind her. The fire beings engulfed Fear, and it was gone in a cloud of smoke.

CHAPTER 14

Reunion

NEVAEH FELT LIKE SHE WAS FLOATING as she threw open her front door and went bounding inside. She couldn't believe what had just happened. All her fear of riding was gone! She was learning so much from her aunt and Sera. She couldn't wait to see what happened next.

"Where have you been?" Lily yelled at Nevaeh as soon as she was through the door. "You were only supposed to ride for an hour. It's four o'clock! You've been gone all day!"

"We never even rode. I've just been with Aunt Celeste and my friends all day," Nevaeh explained, trying to calm her mother down.

"That is no excuse! You live here, not there! Is that understood?" Lily hollered at Nevaeh. "Is that understood?" She hollered again when Nevaeh didn't respond.

"Yes," Nevaeh whispered as she turned to run up the stairs to her room.

"Dinner is at six. Don't be late," Lily called after Nevaeh.

Nevaeh burst through her bedroom door and collided with something. "What on earth?" Nevaeh thought.

"Whoa there, tiger," Alister said, catching Nevaeh just before she hit her floor.

"Ali!" Nevaeh could barely believe what she was seeing. Just a few days before this she wouldn't have believed it.

"Aven!" Ali said as Nevaeh wrapped her arms around him.

"I've missed you so much," Nevaeh said, her face buried in the big angel's chest.

"I heard Lily yelling at you. Are you okay?" Ali asked, concerned.

"She still hates me, Ali. I know she does." Nevaeh allowed herself to feel the pain. She knew she was safe with Ali.

"Have you asked Christos about it?" Ali asked, kissing Nevaeh's head.

"No."

"Maybe it's time you did," Ali suggested.

"Okay," Nevaeh said. She and Alister sat on Nevaeh's bed. Ali held Nevaeh in his strong arms. Nevaeh closed her eyes and began, "Christos, I need to ask You a question."

Instantly, Aven was in her forest.

"Welcome back, brave warrior," Christos said.

Aven turned around. Christos was still the Lion. She walked to Him and buried her face in His mane. Peace overcame Aven, and for a moment she forgot why she'd come.

"I'm so proud of you for dealing with Fear, Aven. That was very brave. Now, I believe you need to ask Me something?" Christos gave Aven a nudge with His nose.

"It doesn't matter anymore. Nothing matters when I'm here with You." Aven meant every word she said.

"I'm glad you are at peace when you're with Me. If you want to carry this peace back with you to the Realm of Earth, you must ask Me your question," Christos advised Aven.

Aven didn't want to ask. She didn't want this moment to end. But she knew Christos was right. She spoke, but it was barely a whisper, "Why doesn't my mom love me?"

"There is someone you should talk to."

Aven followed Christos' gaze. Walking along the river towards them was a young man. Aven guessed he was about fourteen. He looked just like her father. He had the same face, the same light brown hair. His eyes were the same shape as David's, but where David's eyes were hazel, his eyes were deep blue.

"Aven, this is your brother, Joe," Christos told her.

"Heya, sis," Joe said, tears in his eyes.

"Joe?" Aven replied in amazement.

"Come here," Joe said reaching towards Aven to embrace her. "Look at you!" He gushed, "You're so beautiful! You look so much like Mom." He laughed. "Look at those thick, dark curls. You have Dad's eyes, though." Joe squeezed her again. "I'm so happy to see you."

"I've missed you so much!" Aven said, but she didn't move. She just held on tightly.

Christos stood close by. Watching the siblings reunite gave Him great joy. After giving them a few minutes, Christos announced: "Joe, Aven has a question."

"What is it, little sis?" Joe said, sitting down and pulling her to him.

"Why doesn't Mom love me?" Aven did not like needing to ask Joe that question.

"What?! Where did you get that idea?" Joe was shocked that Aven could think such a thing.

"She wishes I were you. She hates me. I'm not good enough. I brought her pain and I didn't mean to." Aven couldn't feel the full weight of her pain here in her forest, but she felt enough of it to make her cry.

"Aven, that's not true. Mom was so excited when she found out you were coming. She literally kicked me out of my bedroom to make a room for you. She moved me into a different room so she could redo the nursery. I remember her dancing through the house, singing. She couldn't wait to have a girl—to have you. Why do you think she named you 'Heaven'?" Joe asked.

"Heaven? She didn't name me Heaven. My name is Nevaeh," Aven told Joe.

"Listen, I don't know why she changed it, but she had picked out the name Heaven. She used to sing to you all the time. I don't remember all the words but it had your name in it like a hundred times. I remember her saying she felt like she was in Heaven when she found out she was pregnant with you." Joe looked to Christos, knowing He'd know more. "Christos, can You tell us what happened?"

"If Aven is ready to hear the truth and accept responsibility for her part..." Christos looked to Aven.

"I need to know what I did," Aven pleaded with Christos.

"Then I will tell you." Christos came and lay down next to Joe and Aven, placing a paw on Aven's lap. "Aven, remember when you were in Heaven, before you went to the Realm of Earth?"

"No, I don't," she answered.

"Remember," Christos said, breathing into her.

"I remember!" Aven said excitedly as her entire memory came flooding back.

"What did I ask you to do?"

"You asked me to bring love and joy to a family in the earth."

"Yes. Why did I ask you that?"

"You said a family needed the love and joy I carry."

"That's right," Christos told her. "Aven, do you remember the day that Joe died?"

"Yes." Aven cried and buried her face in Joe's shoulder as the pain of that day came flooding back.

"What did you do?" Christos needed her to tell her story.

"I cried out for Joe. I needed him, but he wasn't there. I could feel Mom's pain. All I could feel was pain. I was scared. I curled myself up as tight as I could and decided I wouldn't move until Joe came. But he didn't come. I needed him, and he didn't come." Aven wept. She could feel the pain as though it were happening all over again, but the tears somehow helped. It was like she was releasing her pain through them.

“Do you remember the day you were born?” Christos prodded the girl for just a bit more.

“Yes. I do. You were there.”

“Yes, I was,” Christos assured her. “What happened after you stopped seeing Me?”

“The doctor handed me to Mom. She looked at me and smiled, but I couldn’t feel joy. All I felt was pain and loneliness.” Aven was almost choking on her tears.

“That’s right, Aven,” Christos told her, resting His face against hers.

“It was me. It was all me. It wasn’t Mom—I was the one. I was in so much pain after Joe died. I felt overwhelmed with so much pain that I cut myself off. I didn’t want to feel. I didn’t know where you were anymore. I didn’t want to connect to anyone. I thought I did, but I didn’t really. I was too afraid of losing someone I loved, someone I needed, so I didn’t let myself really love anyone.” Aven started calming down after letting it all off her chest.

“That is your part in it, yes. But that’s not the whole story. Would you like to know more?” Christos asked.

Not sure what more there could be, but knowing she needed to know, Aven nodded.

“I knew that Joe was going to die. Before asking you to go, I knew. It wasn’t My will, but I knew it was going to happen anyway. I knew that Lily and David would need someone to help them through their pain, and I knew you carried enough love and joy to do it. I knew you were needed there and that it would be good for you as well.

"Lily and David were overjoyed when they learned they were expecting you. Lily couldn't wait to hold you in her arms. When Joe died, much like you, Lily shut down. What you felt that day in the womb wasn't just the loss of Joe but also Lily's loss. When Lily shut down, you did, too.

"By the time you were born, Lily was starting to feel again. When she held you in her arms for the first time, she tried connecting with you, but you were both too afraid. She wanted to be a good mother to you but was in so much pain she didn't know how to bring you joy.

"You were the only thing that kept her going. Peace used to wash over her as she watched you giggle when Alister cooed over you. Every time she held you, love washed over her.

"Aven, you believed that you were bad because you weren't Joe. You believed you were responsible for his death. That is a lie! You had nothing to do with his death and just because you weren't able to remove all the pain from your family doesn't mean you didn't bring them love and joy. You did, Aven, and I am so very proud of you."

Aven stayed there, allowing herself to be held by Joe and Christos. After she'd cried herself to peace, she looked at Christos. "Christos, You've helped me with my pain. Can You help Mom, too?"

Christos roared into laughter. "Oh, My love. See, only you would think of others so soon after finding your own peace. I am working on Lily, but she needs to accept My healing as you have done. I am so proud of you: you have shown great courage."

With that, the Lion faded and Christos the Man was seated by her side.

CHAPTER 15

Finally Family

NEVAEH DESCENDED. She was still sitting on her bed, Alister holding her. The peace she'd felt in Heaven had come back with her. Nevaeh rested there in Ali's arms, bathing in the peace her healing had brought. Nevaeh didn't know if anything would change between her mother and herself. She hoped it would, but for now it was enough knowing the truth. She hadn't brought pain and she hadn't killed her brother. For the first time in her life, Nevaeh didn't feel guilty.

Nevaeh heard a familiar voice tell her, "Go downstairs." It wasn't an audible voice, but

Nevaeh was learning to listen to the still, small voice inside her.

"I need to go downstairs. Will you be here later?" Nevaeh asked Ali.

"I'm coming with you," Alister informed her. "I've always been right by your side."

Nevaeh smiled, believing every word he said. It was wonderful having her friend back. She didn't know why she was supposed to go downstairs. She guessed Lily would still be mad at her. She wasn't really looking forward to seeing her mother, but she trusted the voice she'd heard and knew that come what may, it would be for her benefit.

Boldly, Nevaeh marched out of her room to the top of the stairs. Just as she was about to start down them, she heard something. It was something she'd never heard before. Slowly and quietly, Nevaeh made her way to the first floor. Stopping at the bottom, she found the source of the sound she'd heard. It came from a sight she'd never seen before.

Sitting curled up on the couch, crying while holding a picture, was her mother.

"Mom?" Nevaeh asked as compassion for her mother swept over her.

Lily looked up. Tears were running down her face. Her eyes were bloodshot and her nose was running.

"Mom, are you okay?" Nevaeh asked, suddenly more concerned for her mother than she ever had been for herself.

"I'm sorry," Lily sobbed.

Nevaeh ran to her mother, putting her arms around her. Lily dropped the picture of Joe she was holding and pulled Nevaeh onto her lap. The two sat there, Lily rocking Nevaeh as she continued to weep. As they rocked back and forth, Nevaeh could feel her connection to her mother growing stronger.

"I love you so much," Lily sobbed, kissing Nevaeh's forehead.

"I'm sorry, Mom," Nevaeh repented to her mother.

"Sorry for what?" Lily asked, confused.

"I'm sorry about Joe. I'm sorry I couldn't fill that place in your heart and take away your pain. I'm sorry I had to live and he had to die."

"Oh, sweetie!" Lily said, broken. "You had nothing to do with your brother's death. It was an accident. I've always blamed myself. If I had been there a moment sooner, perhaps I could have saved him. I was afraid of losing you, too. For the longest time, I had nightmares about you dying."

"I felt like you wished I was dead. Well—that I'd never been born, at least." Nevaeh couldn't believe how easy she now found sharing her feelings with her mother.

"Never! I loved you so much, right from the first moment I held you. I was still in so much pain from Joe's death, but I loved you. I remember holding you for the first time. All I could think about was how much it would hurt to lose you. I should have been thinking about how wonderful it was to hold you, but I was so afraid. I'm so sorry I let my fear hold me back from rejoicing over you the way I should have."

"I remember feeling your pain. I was in pain, too. I loved Joe and felt his death. All I wanted to do was stop you from hurting. I felt like if I could remove your pain, mine would leave, too." Nevaeh shared her heart with her mother.

"Baby, no one could have removed my pain. But you did ease it. You were such a good baby. You were always laughing and giggling. I remember watching you when you giggled. It always made me feel like everything was right with the world. I wanted to connect with you so badly. You were the only thing that kept me going. If it hadn't been for you, I don't know how I would've survived."

"I always felt so alone. I didn't think you loved me." Tears welled up in Nevaeh's eyes, but the sting of the memory was gone.

"I'm so sorry you felt that. Everything seemed upside down. Nothing made sense and I was mad at God. I completely turned my back on Him. I even changed your name," Lily confessed.

"What was my name supposed to be?" Nevaeh knew the answer, but she wanted to hear it from her mom.

"Heaven. I was going to name you Heaven. But then when Joe died, it was like everything inside me twisted. 'Nevaeh' is 'Heaven' spelled backwards, and it seemed to fit. At the time, everything felt backwards to me," Lily finished with a sigh. It felt like the weight of the world had been lifted from her shoulders.

Nevaeh didn't move from her mother's lap, and Lily continued to rock Nevaeh, humming a tune that was vaguely familiar to Nevaeh. Somehow, it felt like Nevaeh was a baby again. It felt like they had a fresh start and they were bonding just as a mother bonds with her newborn child.

Dinner that night was like nothing Nevaeh had ever experienced. For the first time in her life, she felt like a part of the family. She didn't understand exactly what had happened, but not only had her relationship with her mother been restored, she now felt connected to her father. Even little Joy was a joy to be around.

"I think I'll open the pool next weekend," David said, looking at Nevaeh. "It will be too cold to swim for a little bit yet, but this way I can have it ready for when it gets warm enough."

“Maybe the first warm weekend of the summer you can have Liam and Sera over for a pool party,” Lily added.

“Can I come?” Joy asked, batting her eyes at Nevaeh. Joy was the spitting image of Lily.

Nevaeh laughed. How had she not just loved these people before? They were her family, after all.

The following morning, Nevaeh eagerly joined her family at the breakfast table. Lily didn’t make oatmeal.

“I promised Joy I’d take her to the pet store. We need dog food,” David said, helping clear the dishes after breakfast. “Want to come, Nevaeh?”

“I think I’ll stay home with Mom.” Nevaeh loved the pet store, but there were still a few things she wanted to talk to her mom about.

“Suit yourself,” David said, ruffling Nevaeh’s hair.

After the dishes were all done, David packed Joy up in the car and headed to the pet store.

“Mom, can we talk?” Nevaeh asked as soon as they were alone.

“Of course, sweetie. What do you want to talk about?” Lily asked, taking Nevaeh’s hand and leading her to the couch.

"What happened between you and Aunt Celeste?"

Lily closed her eyes. "Nothing," Lily hesitated. "Nothing at all. Celeste used to be my best friend. I was so excited for her when she had that first offer out in Texas. When she came home, I was about six months pregnant with you. It was so good to see her. I'd missed her so much."

Nevaeh knew there was more to the story. "But you didn't speak to her for years. Even now you aren't close."

"I know," Lily took Nevaeh's hand. "That's something I need to speak to her about."

"Will you tell me what happened?" Nevaeh pressed.

Lily sighed. "I really need to talk to your aunt about this, but I think you're old enough to understand. We were raised as believers. Your aunt was always closer to Christos than I was, but I loved Him, too, and had a relationship with Him. When Joe died, I lost my faith. I was mad at God. I felt like He'd taken my son away from me." Lily paused again. She was having a hard time talking about it. "After Joe's funeral, some people came to the house. Celeste was here, too. At one point, I couldn't take it anymore and I fell to the floor, crying. Your aunt was the first one there. She grabbed me and held me. It felt so good to be held by someone I knew loved me." Lily started crying.

"Then she said it. Your aunt told me, 'God will work it for good.' I lost it. I was so mad at God and so mad at her for daring to talk to me about Him when I was so mad at Him. I told her to get out of my house—I never wanted to see her again.

"She tried calling me several times over the next few weeks, but I refused to speak to her. I was in so much pain and I just wanted to hold onto my pain. I felt like I would be betraying Joe if I let go of it.

"I considered reaching out to her after you were born. Before I did, your Grandma Matilda told me that she'd been offered a full-time job in Texas and had taken it. My baby sister had moved halfway across the country to follow her dream. I had been so mad at her that I didn't even know it. I realized at that point that I'd ruined our relationship for good. I'd lost my best friend and all she'd done was try to help me through the death of my child." Lily was sobbing by this point. "I miss her so much."

Just then there was a knock on the door.

"Nevaeh, could you please get that, so I can go fix my face quick?" Lily kissed Nevaeh on the head and headed towards the bathroom in hopes of disguising the fact that she'd just been crying.

Nevaeh opened the door to her Aunt Celeste. "Hi, Aunt Celeste. What are you doing here?" Nevaeh asked. She had a sneaking suspicion she knew.

"Hi, sweetie. I heard your mom wants to talk to me," Celeste said, squeezing Nevaeh's soulder tenderly.

"We were just talking about you." Nevaeh smiled. She loved how Christos worked. The moment she was ready to face her fear, He was there. And now, the moment Lily was finally ready to let go of her pain and reconcile with her sister, Celeste showed up on the doorstep. Nevaeh was beginning to realize that we very seldom have to wait on Christos. He is almost always waiting on us.

"I know you were, Vay. That's why I'm here. Can you please go ask if she's ready to see me?" Celeste waited by the door. She knew Lily was ready. She'd been told. But she also knew it was important that Lily said it and chose to invite her in.

After a few moments, Lily emerged from the bathroom, followed by Nevaeh, and made her way to the living room. Celeste was still standing by the front door. Seeing her sister standing in the doorway brought Lily back to a time when Celeste wouldn't have even bothered to knock. The sisters were so close that they never would have considered knocking. They'd both just walk right in and make themselves at home in the other's house. They were family and best friends. They shared everything. So, the sight of Celeste waiting to be invited in broke something inside of Lily. She wanted things to go back to the way they had been.

"Come in. Make yourself at home," Lily said, choking back tears.

The sisters sat at opposite ends of the couch.

It was Celeste who spoke first. "I'd like to apologize to you." Everything in Celeste wanted to reach out to her sister, to hold her.

"Celeste, you don't need to." Tears spilled over onto Lily's cheeks as she spoke.

"No, please," Celeste needed to be heard. "I shouldn't have said it. I knew you were struggling. I was just trying to help, but I now realize that it was insensitive. I didn't know what to say. I shouldn't have said anything. I should have just been there for you. I should have just loved you and let Papa deal with your heart."

"I know you were only trying to comfort me. I was mad at God, not at you. I felt like He'd taken my son from me and you were questioning my faith. I'm so sorry. I love you." Lily reached towards Celeste who was instantly in her arms.

"I'm so sorry you felt like I was judging you," said Celeste.

"I knew you weren't really judging me. I was judging myself. I'd been trying to tell myself that

God would work it for good, but I could feel myself slipping. When you said those words to me, it felt like a slap in the face. I'm sorry I didn't reach out to you sooner. I've missed you so much. I've missed so much of your life. Let me look at you." Lily pulled away from Celeste, but kept her hands on her little sister's shoulders. "You are so beautiful, and I'm so proud of you for following your heart and pursuing your dreams. I'm so sorry I wasn't there for you."

"I missed you every day. I can't tell you how many times I wanted to call you to share something with you. I've never stopped loving you or wanting to be a part of your life." Celeste was overjoyed to finally be having this conversation with Lily, and to be near her beloved niece as well.

Lily opened her arms towards Nevaeh, who had been listening to her mother and aunt from across the room. The three of them sat on the couch talking for hours. Celeste had waited for over eleven years for this moment, always knowing that one day they would be reunited.

Finally, the day had come.

CHAPTER 16

The Beginning

NEVAEH STOOD AT THE ARENA GATE with Sera and Liam. Demi and Ember were all saddled. Celeste and Jim held the horses, waiting for the girls.

"You don't need to do this, Vay," Liam told Nevaeh. "I know you're still scared. You have nothing to prove. Just because your aunt gave you a horse doesn't mean you need to ride it."

"Liam, I told you—I'm not afraid anymore," Nevaeh assured Liam.

He still didn't believe her.

"Ready when you are, girls," Celeste called to Nevaeh and Sera.

Nevaeh walked over to Demi. She held the reins and mane with her left hand. With her right, she grabbed the back of the saddle. She placed her left foot into the stirrup and without hesitation she pulled herself up, swung her right leg over Demi's back, and settled herself into the saddle.

"Well done, Nevaeh," Sera said, waiting for her turn to mount.

"Yes, well done," Celeste agreed with Sera. "Come on Sera, your turn."

The girls' first lesson went incredibly well. It was as if they had both been riding for years. They were both confident in the saddle and had what Celeste called a "good seat."

"Girls, you help Jim brush the horses down and put them out in the pasture. Liam, you can come help me make sandwiches. Girls, when you're done, meet me and Liam under the weeping willow for a picnic." Celeste turned to go inside, Liam at her heels.

It didn't take long to put the horses out, and soon Nevaeh and Sera joined Celeste and Liam under the tree.

"I still can't believe you rode," Liam told Nevaeh as soon she sat down.

"I told you—I'm not afraid anymore," Nevaeh said, exasperated.

"That doesn't make sense to me," Liam said, clearly unsure of what had been happening right under his nose. "You were terrified the other day."

"Christos helped me conquer my fear. It's dealt with," Nevaeh said, smiling as she spoke about Christos.

"I know that's what you said, but I don't understand how that can happen," Liam said, wanting to understand.

Celeste joined the conversation: "Like I said the other day, it's easier to show you than to tell you."

Sera winked at Nevaeh. "I think you're starting to come around," she said to Liam.

"It's not that I don't believe you. I'm just afraid to see," Liam admitted.

"So was I," Nevaeh said. "I was afraid of so many things, but Christos helped me. I'm sure if you asked Him to, He'd help you, too."

"Why would He help me?" Liam asked, sounding defeated.

"Because He loves you," Nevaeh said.

"How do you know He loves me?" Liam questioned.

"Because I remember playing with you in Heaven before we came here. Christos loved and trusted you enough to send you. It's an honor being sent here. You trusted Him enough to say 'yes' when He asked you." Nevaeh was starting to sound like Celeste and Sera.

"You remember what?" Liam was shocked, but something inside him told him it was truth.

"I remember playing with you in Heaven. You were one of my best friends," Nevaeh repeated.

The second time Nevaeh said it, something woke up inside of Liam. He said, "Tell me more."

"Well I really only know my story. But we could go ask Christos to show you yours." Nevaeh's spirit was leaping inside her as she spoke.

"Go where?" Liam asked, almost breathless. He felt a shift inside and something seemed to be pulling him up.

"Back to the place we chose life. Back to The Tree." Nevaeh could feel it, too. It was as if a vacuum had opened up above their heads and was drawing them up.

"I don't know how." Liam was shaking as his spirit awoke and unfolded itself.

Nevaeh wasn't exactly sure how to go about it either, but the pull upwards was getting stronger every second.

"Just look up and let go," Sera spoke soothingly.

Liam and Nevaeh both looked up and let go of their doubts.

"Where are we?" Liam asked, looking around.

Aven gasped. She knew this place and she loved it well. "We're home!"

As Liam continued to look around, flashes of memories came flooding back. "The river!" he exclaimed, running towards it. "Aven, do you remember the river?" he gushed.

"Race you to the bottom," Aven challenged, grinning from ear to ear and diving in, Liam right behind her.

As Aven reached the bottom, she gracefully spun and came to rest on the soft bed of the river. "Join me?" she asked Liam, who was struggling with the fact that in this place they could breathe underwater. Or maybe the need to breathe at all had gone. Still, he followed Aven's lead and lay down, looking up through the water.

"Aven?" Liam didn't know how to ask what he needed to.

"What is it Liam?" Aven asked, releasing the tiger fish she had been holding.

"I remember being here. I remember how life was here before we left this place." Liam paused, not sure how to express what he was feeling.

"So do I. I remember lying here just like this watching the light dance like it's doing now. I love this place—there is no other place like it," Aven said as a herd of seahorses swirled around them, playfully stirring the waters and causing a whirlpool that sent Aven's hair spinning upwards. As the current from the whirlpool reached the surface, it turned into a waterspout that began prancing about. Aven could feel herself being swept up in this paradise.

"Do you think Christos lied to us?" Liam felt ashamed to even be asking. He felt like a failure.

Aven closed her eyes and thought about her answer. She knew the lie Liam was referring to. She had felt it, too. "No," Aven answered as peace rose within her. "I used to. I used to wonder how Christos tricked me into going to the Earth Realm. To be completely honest, there was a time I hated Him for it." Aven bowed her head as thankfulness swept over her. She looked at Liam, who still looked hurt and confused. "I remember thinking that if Christos had been honest with me, I never would have agreed to go. I felt so alone and afraid. I felt like He had abandoned me. I thought He hated me. Why would I have ever agreed to such pain?"

"That's how I still feel," Liam admitted. "If Christos didn't lie to you, why did you go?"

"Because I trusted Christos and wanted to be closer to Him." Aven could tell her answer hadn't satisfied Liam. "Liam, my journey is my own. I know my story and my reasons, but I don't think it's my story or my reasons you need to hear."

"I can't just stay here forever, can I?" Liam sighed with longing.

"No, you can't. There is no going back, only forward." Aven took Liam's hand. "I think you should talk to Christos about how you're feeling."

"I can't, Aven. I can't tell Him I think He lied to me." The thought horrified Liam.

"You can if that's the truth," Aven assured him.

Liam looked into Aven's face. He could find no sign of judgment or disgust. "Okay," he consented.

Aven and Liam swam to the surface together. Reaching the bank, they climbed out of the river. Hand in hand, they walked to The Tree. There they found Christos.

"I've been waiting for you, Liam," Christos said, motioning for Liam to sit beside Him. "You wanted to speak to Me?" Christos asked—but it wasn't really a question.

Lowering his head with shame, Liam accused Christos, "You lied to me!"

"When did I lie to you?" As Christos spoke, Liam could feel the kindness in His voice wrapping itself around him.

"I don't remember." Liam felt like a fool as he said it.

"Oh," Christos said calmly. "Then how did I lie to you?"

Liam wanted to hide himself under a rock as he answered, "I don't remember."

Christos reached out to lift Liam's chin until the two of them were looking into each others' eyes. "Liam, may I show you something?"

"Yes." Liam's anger was melting away.

Christos reached into Himself and pulled out a scroll. Handing it to Liam, He invited him to open it.

Liam opened the scroll. Wind burst from within it engulfing Liam, pulling him in. Liam found himself at the top of a spiraling staircase. The wind that had carried Liam into the scroll then entered a man who appeared suspended in the center of the staircase. The man opened his eyes. A Being that radiated pure white light stood by the man. Liam heard the Being greet the man: "Hello, Adam." Then the scene faded just as quickly as it had appeared.

With no other way to go, Liam chose to begin his descent. No sooner was the decision made than the same wind swept Liam up and began to carry him, now spinning him downward. As Liam was carried, he continued to watch as scenes from his family's lineage flashed before his eyes.

He could see giants roaming the earth in a time when the wickedness of men was great. A flood came, washing the land of its evil. Men intent on pursuing their own goals built a tower. Before the tower was completed, the same wind that carried Liam swept through the men, confusing them. A new form of speech entered the men and they began to babble, unable to communicate. He saw a shepherd boy in a field. A clash of swords instantly pulled his attention from the shepherd boy to a battle. He saw knights falling, kingdoms collapsing. Suddenly, he heard gunshots and men dropped like flies. A little boy who looked just like Liam was standing in front of him, tears leaving white trails down the cheeks of his soot and ash-stained face.

Liam saw himself standing under a tree with Christos and Aven. Only a moment later, Liam was dropped onto a landing. The scene that unfolded before Liam's eyes sent shivers of hope and pulses of might through his entire body. Liam stood, sword in hand, holding the head of a...

With his scroll glowing in his hand, Liam was once again with Christos under The Tree. "I remember," Liam whispered, gasping as the full weight of his destiny caved in on him. "I remember everything."

"Did I lie to you?" Christos gently prodded Liam.

"No!" Liam froze as understanding opened his eyes. "You told me I was called to redeem my family's DNA. You never told me it would be easy—You only promised that if I allowed You to make me strong, it would be worth it."

"Will you let Me make you strong?" Christos asked, almost in a growl that awoke purpose inside of Liam.

"Make me strong!" Liam cried. It was his deepest heart's cry. That cry echoed through the Realms, calling the children back to the Earth.

Liam and Nevaeh were once again sitting under the willow with Sera and Celeste. As quickly as they had ascended, they were back. No sooner were they back in the Earth Realm than Liam found himself doubting that anything he'd just experienced had been real.

"What'd He say?" Nevaeh asked Liam. She had been watching his encounter from a distance and hadn't heard what was said.

"I don't know." Rejection and Fear had already begun tightening their grip on Liam.

"Liam, I don't know what Christos told you, but I know that I've been in pain most of my life here until I started listening to Christos and agreed to let Him take away my fear and pain."

"I've seen the change in you, Nevaeh. It's not that I don't want to change. I just don't know how. My life isn't going to get any better. I'm a loser, just like my Dad," Liam reasoned.

"I didn't think my life was going to get any better either, but it did. Why don't you just ask Christos to help you and see what happens? Just trust Him—that's what I did and I can't believe how my life turned out." Nevaeh was bursting with joy.

Liam was ready to change. Not believing anything he'd just experienced had been real, but hoping Nevaeh was right, he said, "Christos, I choose to trust You. I need Your help."

A strong wind blew the branches of the weeping willow apart. Christos walked through the opening. He said, laughing, "Oh, Vay—you can't believe this is how your life turned out? This is still just the beginning!"

With that, Christos reached His hand towards Liam, and they were gone.

ABOUT THE AUTHORS

Amanda Summers has been visiting Heaven for as long as she can remember. She is grateful for parents who encouraged her vision and never told her it was just her imagination.

Amanda has always had a thirst for adventure. At age twelve, while canoeing, she and her family braved their way to safety through a raging flash storm. Her love of travel has allowed her to shop Los Angeles, fly-fish Montana, and ride horseback through the mountains of Wyoming. She was almost kidnapped at the Taj Mahal.

Amanda lives in New York and awaits her next adventure with her dog, Sophie, and cat, Maggie.

Kay Summers homeschooled her four children with a desire to train them up in the ways of Christos, to protect their ability to see and perceive truth, and to have confidence in their own hearts. Her hope is to see a whole generation equipped to trust and live from their hearts—to live from the Kingdom within.

Kay lives with her husband in New York in close proximity to her children and grandchildren.